Forget those Things

Sequel to
"The Evidence of Things Not Seen:
A contemporary novel of a family in
conflict and crisis"

Dr. Shawn Jones Richmond

A GOSHEN PUBLISHERS BOOK

FORGETTING THOSE THINGS
Copyright © 2021 by Dr. Shawn P. Jones Richmond

ISBN: 978-1-7342639-9-2

This book is a work of fiction. Names, characters, businesses,
organizations, places, events, and incidents either are the
product of the author's imagination or are used fictitiously.
Any resemblance to actual persons, living or dead, events, or
locales is entirely coincidental.

For information contact www.DrShawnRichmond.com

Cover design by Goshen Publishers

Published by Goshen Publishers LLC
www.GoshenPublishers.com

10 9 8 7 6 5 4 3 2 1

DEDICATION

This book is dedicated to Calvin.

He believed in me. He encouraged me. He supported me.

He loved me unconditionally.

I hope that from heaven he can see that I am not forgetting those things.

Semper Fi.

Forgetting those Things

Sequel to "The Evidence of Things Not Seen: A contemporary novel of a family in conflict and crisis"

Dr. Shawn Jones Richmond

PROLOGUE

I am not sure when I knew that I would write contemporary Christian fiction. There was not a singular defining moment.

I have always loved books. I read all kinds: biographies, literature, historical fiction, suspense, self-help, and memoirs.

There are some that I re-read because they are entertaining. Some, I do not read from cover to cover, but reference specific sections for topics of interest. Others, I collect because they are interesting or because I am supporting the authors, but I only skim through the pages. There is the Bible, of course. I study it regularly and always find the guidance that I need in it. I recommend that everyone tries it.

What is missing from my library is suspenseful, faith-based, modern, entertaining books. More specifically, contemporary Christian fiction. I would like to read more books that have meaning but are not self-help, and are faith-based but not Bible beating, and are entertaining but not unrealistic. I guess that brings me to a Toni Morrison quote, "If there is a book that you want to read, but it hasn't been written yet, then you must write it."

I think that is what happened. There was not a genre for me, so I created one.

Oh, there is Christian fiction. A quick search on Amazon will reveal many. There are hundreds, or maybe even thousands of popular Christian authors. I belong to their networks and enjoy their writing. I connect with them on social media. I attend their conferences. I buy and read their books.

As a literary agent, I have published dozens of books (fantastic reads, I must admit) for other authors. Many of them are Christians. There are plenty of Bible-based books out there.

That is not quite the point though.

Have you ever met someone who does not fit in a category box? You know, the person who does not have a specific classification or grouping? Is it you? It is me for sure. There are no books (at least none that my search revealed) about people like me.

What do I mean by *people like me?*

I lived 1/2 of my childhood in North Carolina and in church, so I am a southern Christian belle. We send handwritten notes, prepare Sunday dinners with place settings, brew iced tea (sweet, of course!), pray before eating, and practice warm hospitality. We like home cooked food and clean, organized homes. We take pride in beautiful yards and handmade crafts. We have rocking chairs on our front porch. We enjoy sitting under shade trees in the summer. We prefer fresh produce from our own gardens. We are soothed by the sound and smell of rain through open windows. We honor God without ceasing, in church and at home. We dress modestly and with sophistication. We like obedient and well-disciplined children. Manners is everything. Family traditions are sacred.

Having said that, the other 1/2 of my upbringing I lived in Washington, D.C., so I have urban vibes. Our neighborhoods were comprised of clusters of apartment buildings and the residents were like family. We understood that street smarts were necessary for survival and therefore we were a close-knit community with strong relationships.

By the time I was a teenager I was discovering my love of reading. Not surprisingly, it encompassed a combination of inner-city and rural lifestyles. Some story plots contained diverse and dense city populations. Occasionally the authors would take me to the D.C. metropolitan area and mention Georgetown shops and Tysons Malls. Some were set on midwestern farms. The characters would raise cattle, grow food, and shop at small town craft fairs and local convenience stores.

As an adult, we could add in live entertainment. I like sports. I mean, I really like sports! I have spent more money than I care to admit at NBA championships, NFL playoffs, and even a Super Bowl game. If it weren't for the COVID-19 pandemic, I would probably have tickets to a playoff game (or the Super Bowl!) now.

And we are adults so we can talk, right? I am a born again, baptized, Holy Ghost filled, Bible teaching, gospel preaching, Jesus loving, hymn singing, woman of God. And I am super social. And I like to have fun. Oh, and I am single. I was married. Happily so. He was sick and passed away (this book is dedicated to him). I don't know how I feel about remarrying because it changes from week to week. I might. I might not. We'll see how that plays out.

Do you have any idea how unique this combination is: a Christian, extroverted, middle-aged, fun loving, ½ country, ½ city, single (for now) woman? Have you read many books about her?

And since we are talking, I am a career woman. That is probably an understatement. I am a serial entrepreneur. I build businesses. I publish books. I teach. I preach. And because I enjoy it all, I am not ready to give any of it up.

Do you see what I mean?

Who is writing books for *people like me*??

I like to drive my Jeep through the mountains. I also have fun with my sports car on the highways.

Who is writing books for *people like me*??

I cook meat for my family, but I am pescatarian.

Who is writing books for *people like me*??

My life motto is simple: "Broken Crayons Still Color". I believe there is good in every situation.

Who is writing books for *people like me*??

I am.

My characters each have a little of my own truth in them (some more than others). They decide daily to acknowledge the blessings of life, rejoice, and be glad, despite their circumstances. They learn when to love and when to let go. They have the serenity to accept the things they cannot change, and the courage to change the things they can. They regard highly the precious gift of peace.

They are clear on their values and priorities. You will see that theme throughout this book. The characters must choose joy even when it does not choose them.

I will let you get to the story but there is one more thing you should know. While these stories are purely fictional, I have interwoven biblical truth throughout. If you are a Bible scholar, you will pick up on the subtleties. If not, you will probably just appreciate how real the characters are. They are people like me (and perhaps like you, too).

For example, this story includes a new individual. I named her Mattie because she comes from the book of Matthew. I birthed her from Matthew 5:12, 6:12, and 7:12. That is why when you read about Mattie, you will see the number 12 frequently, and it is why I mention "Shen Valley" 12 times. Those Scriptures teach us to (1) treat people the way we would like to be treated even when they do not look like us or live like we do; (2) forgive people who do not know how to love us; and (3) rejoice always because God is great, and God is good.

Another example of Bible-based writing is a frequent reference to green pastures and still waters (similar to this book's cover), and the number 23. That is because those scenes are based on the 23rd Psalm. My goal was to ensure that you do not become so immersed in the family's circumstances that you do not see God's goodness. He is our shepherd, and He is there all the time.

One more? The Apostle Paul wrote letters to the churches at Corinth and Philipi about pressing forward. I named characters from those epistles Paul Cory and Philip Pressley. Get it?

There are biblical allusions throughout the book!

Now that we have cleared that up, "The Evidence of Things Not Seen" (Heb 11:1) was about a family in crisis. The main plot unfolded in three days (Friday to Sunday). You know why, don't you? This book, "Forgetting those Things" (Phil 3:13), the sequel, picks up the story on the very next day. It begins on Monday morning, the day after a resurrection.

Enjoy!

1. OPPORTUNITY

She was still processing the toilsome three-day search and rescue of her best friend when her phone vibrated in her bag. The incoming calls had been nonstop and filled her voicemail. This caller's ID is one that she did not recognize. They had called several times, so she answered. The conversation only lasted 3.13 minutes but would change the trajectory of her life.

On Friday, Ida had left Manhattan to drive down to Shenandoah Valley, Virginia, for Patty's retirement celebration. They had been planning for several weeks and were looking forward to it. The event occurred that same evening shortly after she arrived, launching the mission that concluded somewhat successfully on Sunday. Having spent Sunday night in the hospital waiting room with the family and receiving both good and bad news while still there on Monday, she was not prepared for the phone call.

Dr. Shawn Jones Richmond

You will recall that she began working as an Electronics Engineer 20 years ago and still finds her career gratifying, so she is certainly not looking for a work change. She is happy with her job and has rightfully earned but graciously passed on many job offers over the past couple of decades. They were all for executive leadership opportunities, which many people would have wanted. Ida is not like many people.

The only offer of advancement she had accepted was that shift from Junior- to Senior Design Engineer, 15 years ago. And she only accepted that one because it came with the freedom to be more innovative. *Freedom.* That is the word that probably best describes Ida. There might be others that pertain to her lifestyle as well: independence, nonconformity, and unconventionality. But if you asked her, for now, she would agree with *freedom.*

When she designed the special gift for Patty, it was made from her heart and out of necessity. Patty needed a way to track and communicate with her beagle, Rosie, who would venture off during their mountain runs, and then get lost.

The invention had been instrumental during the crisis and, consequently, publicly reflected Ida's unique talents. She designs electronics that solve everyday problems, and her dozens of copyrights showcase her originality. The general public, however, was completely unaware of her skills, until now.

Ida designed and manufactured a new prototype of a bracelet and dog collar to address Patty's problem. When Rosie, would run off in pursuit of squirrels, raccoons, and rabbits, Patty could communicate through the bracelet on her wrist, with the matching collar on Rosie.

Ida, the most creative when it came to electronics, did not stop with the design that worked flawlessly. She also personalized both products with etchings and engravings that made them aesthetically appealing. They were tools and yet they were jewelry. Little did Ida know when she designed the set, that the same weekend that she delivered it to Patty, it would be the essential apparatus for finding and saving her.

Patty's father, the Retired United States Marine Corps Lieutenant General, Reverend Patrick Lewis Harris, Sr. (yes, that's a mouthful, so let's just call him Rev. Harris), had devised a plan whereby calls to Patty were broadcasted over the site where a college structure had collapsed on her during an earthquake.

When Patty heard her name called out, she was able to respond via her bracelet, compliments of Ida. She pressed a button that signaled Rosie who eventually led the group to her exact location. What is even more impressive is that, once they were close enough, Patty could speak into the microphone built into her bracelet and the search team near Rosie could hear her responses through the speaker on her dog collar.

The entire nation had watched as a news helicopter broadcasted the mission live. Marines and church parishioners who had served under or alongside Rev. Harris watched in admiration as their trailblazer led the charge. Patty's track mates from high school and college, and students she taught at the community college watched in angst. The world watched and prayed for the kind lovely lady who had been trapped under the wreckage of a collapsed building.

When Ida's phone rang, it was from the office of another retired USMC General who had commanded alongside Rev. Harris. He had a strikingly similar personality. He, too, was uncompromising, demanding, and impersonal.

She answered the call from the hospital waiting room where Patty's family was rejoicing that Patty had survived the accident, but they were lamenting the news of Lewis, her brother, who had died from complications of lung cancer the day before. They were still awaiting updates of Patty's recovery from numerous critical surgeries.

"Hello."

"Hello. Are you Ida Wilson?"

"Yes, I am."

"I am Major Paul Cory. Please hold for General Philip Pressley."

"Who?" She didn't recognize the number on her phone, nor the voice of the person who spoke so quickly that she did not catch his name, *Major 'Somebody'* for a *General 'Somebody'*.

He slowed his speech as he repeated, "Lieutenant General Philip Pressley, Ma'am. Please hold."

A few seconds later, a slightly unpleasant and somewhat intimidating voice came on the line, "Ms. Wilson?"

"Yes?"

"Good Morning. Thank you for taking my call. I am General Pressley of the United States Marine Corps, retired."

"What can I do for you, Sir?"

I served with Rev. Harris. I know him well. Along with our watchful nation, I tracked the mission for his daughter, Patricia. I am glad she was located. I knew that with her father leading the charge, victory was inevitable. And, I must say that I am impressed with your tracking devices. Good work."

"Thank you." Not fully recognizing her own brilliance, she was still quite humble. "But it's just a bracelet and a dog collar."

"The reason for my call, Ms. Wilson, is to inquire about the patents for your designs. Do you own them?"

"Yes, I own the patents for both devices."

"Excellent. I have a proposition for you. I retired from the Marine Corp; however, I consult for them in the area of electronics engineering. I would like to bring you on board to address our need for devices that enhance tracking and communicating with service members in combat."

"I'm sorry. I don't understand."

He continued. "Leaders need to be able to communicate during combat with members who are often dozens of miles apart. They also need to be able to track their locations and record their communications and to do so discretely."

She was flattered but, as with the countless other opportunities that had presented over the years, she was not interested. "Thank you but I am not looking for a job at this time."

General Pressley ignored her response and concluded the conversation with, "My deputy is coming back on the line to set up the appointment. Good day, Ms. Wilson."

"Wait, what?"

"Ma'am?" Major Cory continued the conversation.

"Yes?"

"We will make your travel arrangements. Please be prepared to report to Twenty-Nine Palms, California, in seven days.

"California?" She was appalled at their resolute insistence. "I just told the other guy that I am not interested in a job."

"Yes, Ma'am. Your presence is requested at the Marine Corps Communication and Electronics School, commonly referred to as MCCES."

Admittedly, that was somewhat intriguing to Ida. "What goes on there?"

"Ma'am, we train Marines in electronics and tactical communications. Our mission is to ensure that Marine commanders at all levels have the ability to exercise command and control across the full range of military operations."

That one line contained all the buzzwords of her career. The hook for her was *tactical communications.* "Am I only coming to meet? Are there any requirements? Does my attendance represent any commitment?"

"No, Ma'am. It is just a discussion, Ma'am."

"In seven days? Then, in her rapid speech, she responded in a single breath, "Because I have to be back on the east coast for Lewis' funeral and depending on how Patty recovers she may need me here, and I have to go home to Manhattan first and pack, and I need to grab my design sketches and development codes."

"Yes, Ma'am, with General Pressley. We will be in touch again with your travel arrangements. We assume you prefer to fly out of LaGuardia Airport or JFK International Airport."

"Yes. How'd you know that?"

He chuckled but did not answer the question. "Thank you, Ma'am. We will be in touch again soon."

It could be because she hadn't had a good night's sleep since Thursday, but the guy on the phone actually sounded kind of enchanting. She would have Googled him, but she could not remember his name.

She did remember "MCCES", so she searched the Internet for it, and to her pleasant surprise, there it was on their website, exactly what Major *What's-His-Name* had said: "... train Marines in ground electronics maintenance, tactical communications, ... exercise command and control across the full range of military operations".

She could not believe that there is an entire military training command with multiple schools, for electronics. How cool will it be to tour the Marine Corp's electronics labs?!

Enthralling. So, she'd go.

2. EMERGENCE

At 6:14 AM, Patty awakened. After the various surgeries yesterday, including the one on her brain, today would be critical.

Her hospital room was quiet at first. The fluorescent light in the ceiling was still off from the night before. The medical alert systems and monitors were all silent except for an occasional beep on the intravenous drip machine.

In stark contrast to her warm and cozy mountain cottage, her hospital room smelled and looked sterile. The air was filled with the wafting of cleansers, disinfectants, and sanitizers. Void of any personal affects, there was schematic light blue décor throughout the room, accentuating the coordinated pattern of the wall, bed, floor, and chairs. Any semblance of her home would not have mattered much anyway because she could not see them. Her head was immobilized to prevent additional injury.

Her intensive care unit room was on the eastside of the hospital and, thankfully, with a spectacular view. That, for sure, she appreciated. Three large windowpanes connected to make one huge window out of the entire wall. Knowing that Patty loved to start her day, every day, catching the sun as it began to peek over the cascading hills of the Blue Ridge Mountains, her family had requested to move her hospital bed and position her so that she could awaken to her favorite sight.

That morning, as she peered out of her second-floor window, she saw dewy grass, lots of it, 23 acres of moist, dark green meadow. Off in the distance, as far as the view would allow, she could see an outline of the mountains. It looked as if an artist had used colorful pencils to draw the hills with peaks and dips against the backdrop of the sky.

The sun was just about to make its appearance, rising from the other side of the mountains. *How cool would it be to photograph that sunrise,* she thought. Its affect was widespread, coloring the sky with colors of salmon, orange, and yellow. Other than telephone poles and wires scattered throughout the field, there was nothing to obstruct her view or prevent her from enjoying the scene.

Her eyes were moving from side to side taking in the panorama when they zoomed in closer to a tree just outside her window. It was in the corner, a large mature shade tree. Underneath it, whitetail deer were grazing. Occasionally, two or three of them would suddenly take off with long leaps across the field to where the rest of the herd foraged. Patty was entertained by their playfulness.

When they had all moved away, there remained a large one. It was little over 3 ft tall and probably weighed 200 lbs. It was observant. Frequently, it would stand still with its ears pointed forward and stare at something. It appeared to be on guard, protective of the smaller ones.

The mother, Patty surmised. It had to have been the mother because a tiny, frail deer, certainly a newborn, moved tentatively in stride with her. The mother moved slowly allowing the fawn to keep close as they traversed the green pastures. Patty contemplated, *Why is it so heartwarming to see a mother patiently guide her young, particularly a fragile one?*

It was the morning following her rescue from the college wreckage. On Friday evening, she had gone back to the closed community college to retrieve music sheets she had unintentionally left there. That is when it happened. She was in the building alone when an earthquake caused it to collapse and bury her beneath debris.

Fortunately, Ida had made the bracelet and dog collar, and Patty's father and fiancé had organized a crew of local volunteers to save her. The whole country was praying for her and mercifully God spared her life.

Here she lay in the hospital, having had a large metal shard surgically removed from her head. Her hands were cut so severely that they required numerous sutures. Both of her legs were broken in multiple places.

The doctors had informed her family that the first night would be the most critical, and that they desperately wanted her to wake up the following morning. And now, she has.

A nurse just came to check on Patty and has delightedly found her awake. She immediately called for a doctor, who quickly verified that she was in fact alert and responsive.

He was pleased that she responded to voices and sounds. He was encouraged that, while immobilization prevented head movement, her eyes followed the healthcare workers as they moved about her room.

He instructed a nurse to inform the family of the good news. "The Harris family is still in the waiting room. Please tell them that she is awake. Let them know that many tests must be run immediately but, briefly, very briefly, they can see her."

Patty's legs were no longer suspended in the air with cables and slings. They were however bandaged from her waist down, only revealing her toes. Her arms lay motionless at her sides. Her head was completely wrapped in medical gauze and it was turned to one side, toward the window, in a stabilizer. The massive heap of gauze in the back protected the area where the metal shard had been removed.

There were tubes in her mouth, nose, and both her arms. From underneath her blankets there were more, including catheters for drainage.

Her mother, Evelyn, was her first visitor. She leaned over to Patty's ear and whispered, "Patricia, it's Mother. I am here, Dear. You survived. You're strong and you are a survivor. I love you."

Patty blinked but did not speak.

Her father was waiting just outside her room, but he did not enter. He still could not.

Next, a handsome gentleman named Ned, with trembling hands and eyes that had puffed from another all-night cry, held her hand and spoke to her with endearing expressions. He mentioned picking out a ring and setting a date.

She still did not speak, and she appeared to be puzzled. *My fiancé, perhaps?*

Then a woman younger than the first came in to visit. It was Ida. She said that they were best friends, college roommates and sisters, but Patty did not acknowledge her.

Finally, there was one more woman who visited. She looked and sounded a lot like the first woman. She wanted to share deep family secrets that they had recently discovered but would return later to do so. It was Estelle but Patty did not respond to her either.

After all those visits Patty still had not spoken a single word. Her family assumed that the tube down her throat was most likely preventing speech. They did not think any more of it.

If she were able, she would have asked many questions because it was all so confusing. She did not recognize any of those people. She would have asked who they were and how they knew her. She would have asked their names. She would have asked them why she was immobilized in a hospital.

The surgeons who addressed her head ordeal were astounded that she had survived the trauma. In a four-hour operation, they successfully removed the metal scrap that had lodged six inches through her skull, without rupturing a major artery. They needed to know what damage, if any, might require immediate consideration.

The tests lasted all day and included detection or diagnosis of additional cerebral contusions and lacerations. They wanted to rule out the possibility of extensive damage to her brain tissue. They also tested for intracranial hematomas, blood vessels that may have ruptured within her brain or between her skull and her brain. They examined her for pseudoaneurysms, a collection of blood that would have formed between the two outer layers of an artery, the muscularis propria and the adventitia. It would not have been uncommon because the penetrating metal shard could have injured a vessel, which would then bleed, but form a space between the above two layers, rather than exiting the vessel. And, finally, the neurosurgeons ordered immediate tests for arteriovenous fistulas, an abnormal connection or passageway between an artery and a vein.

Following the neurological examinations, her orthopedic surgeons ordered their battery of tests as well. They had implanted metal screws and rods to reset her legs. Because her legs were incredibly strong, a runner's legs, they were convinced that she would regain use of them but needed to view the surgical areas to verify the realignment. The metal implants prevented MRI (magnetic resonance imaging) scans, so instead they ordered all other scans that would give views to her newly reset multi-fractured legs: x-rays, bone scans, CT (computerized tomography) scans, and PET (positron emission tomography) scans.

Her surgical team unanimously agreed to hold off on testing her other physical symptoms for the time being. It was more important to keep her immobilized until the first set of results were back. Later on, they could measure other issues such as the amount of weakness she experienced when moving her arms, legs, body, and head.

They would also expect Patty to have difficulty sitting, standing, balancing, walking, and changing position in bed, but those measurements could wait as well.

By Tuesday morning, the next examinations were ordered to assess her cognitive abilities. Her doctors had concerns about her difficulty remembering, paying attention, or solving problems. They also assessed her emotional and behavioral symptoms, such as difficulty controlling emotions, or changes in her personality. This was a small town after all, and they would know personally if Patty's behavior or temperament changed.

Twenty-three hours later, all the test results were complete, and the doctors had diagnoses for Patty. The family had stayed at the hospital with her since her admittance on Sunday morning. The thought of going home to freshen up or rest never occurred to them. They dozed off in the waiting room and made the best of the hospital accommodations. They also were comforted from the generosity of Patty's neighbors, Mr. and Mrs. Goodleaf.

A nurse invited the family to join Patty's surgical team in a conference room. The invitation was too formal for the family's comfort. The news must have been ominous. *Why the entire surgical team? Why couldn't the doctors speak with them in the waiting room? Why such formality?* This felt more like a meeting than a status update. It felt fateful. There was surely bad news to follow.

The appearance of the conference room did not help any. It was gloomy. Two or three folding tables had been pulled together to achieve the desired length and accommodate 10-12 people. The rolling chairs were mismatched, perhaps hauled from different offices and waiting rooms to meet the seating requirement. Off in a corner was a rolling cart with refreshments.

Once in the conference room, the family was offered the nourishments. They all declined. They did not want coffee and donuts. They wanted to know what was going on with Patty.

The medical team sat on one side of the table, the family on the other: Rev. Harris, her heroic father, who had prayed desperately for her survival; Evelyn, her poised and composed mother, who had never stopped worrying about her daughter; Estelle, a co-worker who had loved her like family, for an unbelievable reason that she could not wait to share with Patty; Ned, Patty's unrevealed fiancé; Ida, her best friend; and Mr. and Mrs. Goodleaf, her neighbors and dear friends.

The first person on the hospital staff side of the table opened the meeting. She introduced herself as Patty's Case Manager and began with optimism. "The good news", she started, "is that Patty is very strong. She's tough. We are blessed that she's still with us." She paused to take an unusually deep breath before continuing.

We all know that whenever a conversation begins with "The good news is", that there is surely bad news to follow. The Harris family knew that as well.

The Case Manager continued, "We have three different diagnoses. Each doctor will present their case and we are all here to answer your questions and discuss next steps." She looked to the surgeon sitting immediately to her right.

He had as much optimism in his voice as the Case Manager. "First", her Orthopedic Surgeon started, "The resetting of both Patty's legs was successful. I am pleased that her x-rays look great. She will need extensive physical therapy, but we are confident that she will walk again; with a walker at first, then a cane, and eventually without assistance at all. It is possible that she won't even have a limp. It helped tremendously that her legs were in such extraordinary condition prior to the accident."

He then exhaled and looked to the next doctor, the one sitting to his right. They had strategized the order in which they would communicate the results and were speaking in succession. One might surmise that they were beginning with all the good news and helping the family to brace for the most upsetting of the diagnoses.

"Second", her Neurosurgeon began and also with positivity, "there is no immediate evidence of intracranial hematoma. There appears to be significant swelling, which we can treat, but no bleeding in her brain. That is most encouraging. At this point, we do not anticipate additional surgeries. That is extremely encouraging and the best we could hope for. We are expecting that as the swelling subsides, her recovery will improve significantly."

He then dropped his head.

This must be the bad news portion of the report, the entire family thought.

"Next", her Occupational Therapist, the last person in the row on that side of the table, spoke reticently. Her hands were shaking. She paused and nervously flipped through papers in a folder before making eye contact with any of the family members. This was more personal for her. Her son had been one of Patty's students and they all attended the same church. She was a friend. When she began to weep, the Neurosurgeon handed her a handkerchief.

The anticipation was agonizing.

In his distress, Rev. Harris belted out, "Seriously? We have to sit here and await bad news while she blows her nose? This is tormenting. Report already!"

Through quivering lips, she began to explain, "It appears that Patty's cognitive deficits are significant right now."

He interrupted, "We cannot hear you. Speak up."

She continued slightly louder but still emotional and without eye contact. "We will need to conduct more tests and we are hopeful that Patty will make a full recovery. For now, she has an inability to understand what has happened to her and, as a result, she's experiencing noteworthy emotional agitation."

Each loved one seated on the opposite side of the table, looked confounded. *Emotional agitation? What does that mean?* But no one interrupted. Clearly, there was more news.

"In addition, she appears to have no concept of time, her thoughts are jumbled, and she does not remember the earthquake or accident." She paused for another deep breath and then continued.

This time she scanned the row of family members when she spoke, "We showed Patty photos from her social media, of her family and friends and church and Rosie, but she could not identify any of the places nor people in them. And..."

She had to take one more breath before finishing her report, "Finally, she is unable to speak. The part of her brain that controls speech is remarkably damaged right now."

"How significant is her memory loss?" Rev. Harris asked.

"Quite significant, Sir. Both her long-term and short-term memories are compromised."

"Does she know us, her family?" Evelyn inquired.

"I am afraid not, Ma'am. Not yet."

"Will her memory return in time?" Ned asked through his tearfully puffy eyes.

"We hope so, Ned, but honestly, it's too soon to tell. These conditions may change as the cerebral swelling subsides. That is often the case. Rehabilitation therapists will plan to treat many of Patty's symptoms and then we will know more."

With the diagnoses shared, it was the Case Manager's turn to speak again. She began to review the recommended treatment plan. "Physically, Patty is looking great but cognitively there are these areas of grave concern. We recommend transferring her to an acute care center to begin treatment immediately. The sooner she begins, the greater her chances of recovery."

"So, she cannot attend her brother's funeral?" Ida inquired. "Does she even remember that she has a brother?"

"I'm sorry, Ida."

Her Aunt Estelle spoke next, but it was more like she was thinking aloud, "How awful is it to be robbed of all your memories? To not know who you are? She must be terrified."

The Case Manager offered optimism, "There is hope."

"And we do not know *if* her memory will return." Ned was processing the news. "We've made plans. We are engaged to be married. We've been in love all these years. We have dreams. We have a life. She doesn't remember any of it?"

The Case Manager responded sympathetically, "That is correct, Ned. She has forgotten those things."

3. VERACITY

Ralph was driving the Harrises from the hospital and back to Patty's house. They had not driven themselves in years. That was partly because navigating traffic in Manhattan was dreadful, and partly because they could afford the luxury of a full-time dedicated driver, but mostly because Ralph was a reliable friend.

The Harrises rode in silence. The quiet air in the oversized car was filled with the pain of loss.

All of the tragic news had been unbearable. Lewis, their only son, was gone forever. He had died the same day that their daughter, Patty, was rescued. She was alive but, in some sense, was also gone because the head trauma caused her memory deficit and inability to speak.

It was now day six of their nightmare and the couple was maintaining their serenity as best they could. Understandably, they were physically, mentally, and emotionally depleted.

"We must plan a service for Lewis", Evelyn began speaking and barely above a whisper. "We could have his funeral here, in Shen Valley, where he has high school friends. Or, we could have it in New York with his college friends and work colleagues."

Discounting her brainstorming, Rev. Harris replied, "We will have it at New Life Kingdom Church of Christ in Manhattan. That is our home, and his body is already in New York."

She noticed that he said, "his body", and not their son's name. *Was it too uncomfortable to say his name?*

That same Sunday morning that Patty was rescued, Lewis' friend and doctor, GG, had him transported to a trauma center in New York and that's where he subsequently passed away. Because the family had been grieving losing him while they were also anxiously awaiting Patty's medical diagnoses, this evening is the first time they have spoken of Lewis.

They are doing so in the past tense, and it is painful. "I wonder if he wanted anything in particular; if he had any special requests," Evelyn thought aloud.

"He never indicated such to me," Rev. Harris, as stoic as ever.

"Well," she continued, "we must plan a service that will duly honor him."

"Yes, Darling. We must," he agreed.

"There is also something I need to tell you, Patrick."

"Yes?"

"Estelle and I made a shocking discovery while you all were searching for Patricia."

A knot began forming in his stomach. He knew what was coming and dreaded it with every fiber of his being. There was a family secret of which he had been aware, but she had not. He had respectfully honored his promise of confidentiality to her father for the past few decades.

She continued, "When searching for emergency supplies in Patricia's attic, Ida noticed a Bible containing my family's lineage, but it was missing a page. She was curious and asked Lewis if he could use his contacts to conduct a genealogy search. The results came back and are, frankly, amazing."

Looking out of his car window, he did not turn to look at her. He was searching for the right thing to say. He could not lie to her anymore, but he could not push out the words of truth either. All he could muster was, "I know."

Thinking she must have misheard him, "What? What did you say?"

Still turned away from her and toward his car window, "I know."

"Look at me, Patrick."

Slowly, he turned to face her, almost in slow motion. This was the moment he had dreaded all those years. Finally letting go of the burden he had been carrying could be beneficial to his health, both physically and mentally, but it did not feel like it in that car. Keeping secrets had caused stress and anxiety, but nothing like what he felt now. He took a deep breath. He was making an effort to brace himself for what came next.

Her voice was getting louder. "You know what? What do you know?"

He spoke without parting his teeth. Only his lips moved. "I know, Evelyn."

Her heart began racing. "You know what, Patrick?" She was making him say it.

Turned away and looking out his car window again, "I know that you and Estelle are twins and that you were separated at birth."

She was shocked. The questions came out in rapid fire. It was one behind the other and so fast that he did not have time to answer one before the next was coming, "How do you know that? When did you find out? What else do you know? Why won't you look at me?"

Ralph raised the window that separated the front seats from the back in their Mercedes. He knew they would need privacy for this conversation. He was concerned but dared not get involved, so he pretended to be soaking in the beautiful scenery along the hilly and winding roads.

Rev. Harris answered, "I know that Margaret was your stepmother, not your biological mother. John, your father, took you when you were born. Emily, your biological mother, kept and raised Estelle."

She was beyond bewildered and her questions were endless. She released another round. "How do you know this, Patrick? Who told you? How long have you known? Why didn't you tell me? Why are you admitting now that you've known this? Is there more I should know?"

Similar to the situation with the Case Manager back at the hospital, he struggled to explain. He was not as sniffly as her, but he was muttering. "Your father told me years ago when Patricia was in high school. That is why I moved us away so abruptly. And that is why we did not want her to come back here to Shen Valley, for fear that she would discover the truth."

Evelyn had even more questions, "*We*? Who is *we*? The truth? *The* truth? You mean, *her* truth? *My* truth! *Estelle's* truth!"

While he searched for the words to respond, she began to calculate the number of years. "Patricia graduated high school 27 years ago. You have known *my* truth for nearly 30 years? And you never said anything to me about it? You never once felt compelled to inform me of *my* truth in nearly three decades, Patrick?"

Words simply would not come out. He mumbled something.

She mocked him from his response to the Case Manager and belted, "Speak up. I cannot hear you."

He dropped his head and spoke downward toward his lap, "Your father trusted me to safeguard that information, Evelyn."

She turned her full body toward him. "He trusted you? Have you forgotten that I trusted you? I am your wife of nearly 50 years. I trusted you. Have you forgotten that we are a family? We have a 45-year-old daughter. She trusted you. I cannot believe you have deceived us all these years. What else have you concealed? What else do you know? What else have you forgotten?"

He managed to say, "I have not forgotten those things." And then, "Darling, please…"

She interrupted, "Do not 'Darling' me."

She could not believe this was happening. Her eyes welled full. Her chest began to rise and fall rapidly.

He continued to look either downward or out his window, but not at Evelyn.

There was too much to process. The remainder of the ride was quiet. Neither of them spoke again as Ralph turned the vehicle into Patty's driveway.

Evelyn was grieving and confused and angry.

Rev. Harris was lamenting.

Ida and Estelle, oblivious to what had just transpired in the Harrises' car, pulled into the driveway behind them. Given all the sad news they wanted to be of some support to the Harrises. There was much to be done.

They needed to notify acquaintances and make difficult arrangements for both of their children. They had to plan Lewis' funeral. While doing so, they needed to gather paperwork for Patty's admission into an acute care and rehabilitation facility. Estelle and Ida could surely be of assistance.

Ned and the Goodleafs arrived at the same time. As the Chief of Security at the campus where the Patty was injured, Ned needed to go and complete reports for the insurance company, but first wanted to make sure the Harrises were okay. He also had relatives in the area that he needed to visit as they had been texting him to check on Patty's status. He wanted to deliver the news to them in person, so he would not stay long.

The Goodleafs, Patty's loving and rustic neighbors, would return home to unpack the supplies used at the school after the earthquake, and at the hospital during the wait for her surgeries. They would also update their employees at the vineyards who were awaiting news of Patty's condition. But first, they would make sure Estelle, Evelyn, and Ida were aware that they were just a phone call away if any needs arose and that they would check back with them the following day.

They were all brokenhearted. They were all wearied. To make matters worse, they were all unsuspecting of what was about ensue.

Uncharacteristic of Evelyn's custom of walking a half step behind her husband (and in silence), she entered the house first, and with a hurried determination she strutted past the kitchen, through the living room, and stood to the side of the hallway that led to the bedrooms. Pointing down the hall, she shouted to her husband, "You should get your things."

Everyone else had entered the house but none were yet seated. They stood motionless in the living room in disbelief. It is one thing to witness grief but Evelyn, the queen of etiquette, was enraged, and vocally so. She was fuming, and voiced her feelings, loudly.

Evelyn had never expressed anger or even a little dissatisfaction. Not ever. She was the most poised woman they knew. She was always graceful and always dignified. She epitomized high society. Not once had she ever spoken above a whisper. And not once had she spoken in disagreement with her husband, at least not publicly.

This side of her, obviously very expressive and emotional, was one that they had never seen. Evelyn had lost her composure. Yes, Mrs. Evelyn Harris was noticeably agitated and publicly confronting her husband.

Even more stunned was Rev. Harris. His wife had never, ever, in nearly 50 years of marriage addressed him that way. In fact, she would ask his permission before talking in public. And that was a rare occasion because she acquiesced to him speaking on her behalf. He always spoke for the both of them. He decided and he answered for them both, always. She always complied. She respected his position in her life and was honored to submit to him completely.

Until today.

He knew that the horrible pain of them losing their son and then the dreadful news that in some ways they had lost a part of their daughter was excruciating. It was horrendous.

But in his mind, that was a different situation from her learning her family secrets. He wanted to compartmentalize her pain. He tried to separate the emotions of their losses from their reactions to her learning her truth. They were two distinct matters, according to him.

"Evelyn, you are grieving ... ".

She interrupted him in a manner not dissimilar to his own over the past five decades of suspending people mid-sentence. "Yes, I am grieving. And you, you must leave."

Stock-still, Estelle and Ida side glanced each other, barely gesturing at their befuddlement. They had not yet learned why Evelyn was so irate. Their looks inquired of one another; *Do you see what's happening here?* But neither of them moved nor spoke. They acknowledged each other's glances and responded with slight shoulder shrugs.

Ralph had overheard the discussion in the car, so he knew the source of contention. He was also quite clear on Evelyn's directive to retrieve the luggage but wanted to verify with Rev. Harris. He awkwardly asked, "Shall I retrieve the luggage, Sir?"

Evelyn not giving her husband a chance to respond, answered Ralph for him, "Yes, you shall, Ralph and leave mine here. I am staying in Shen Valley until Patricia is recovered. He (pointing to her husband with a jabbing motion) will be returning to New York."

"We need to plan Lewis' funeral, Evelyn." Rev. Harris was still shocked and still speaking through his teeth trying desperately to not raise his voice. "And we need to make rehabilitation arrangements for Patricia."

"I can plan from here, Patrick." Then, pointing toward the luggage that Ralph was retrieving, "You really need to leave now."

His voice was stern but low as he pleaded with her, "Evelyn, please, listen ... "

"Leave, Patrick."

"Evelyn, God would not have us to ... "

Again, she interfered with his pleading but this time, she was beyond maddened. She lost herself in infuriated rage. Her chest was rising and falling rapidly again and this time in rhythm with her heavy breathing. Her eyes narrowed and watered even more. She belted out words, over enunciating with prolonged spacing between them, "DO ... NOT ... PREACH ... TO ME. NOT TODAY, PATRICK HARRIS."

He begged, "Evelyn, please try and understand. I was sworn to secrecy. I made a vow. God would not have me to ... "

She lost it. She walked up to him, tilted her head back slightly so that she could look up into his eyes, and with her whole body shivering, "You will not sermonize your way out of this, Patrick. You will not preach to me about the God who just took our only son; the God who allowed a building to collapse on our only daughter, and then erased her memories and suppressed her speech;

the God who has allowed me to live with a husband who has lied to me for almost 30 years. YOU ... WILL ... NOT ... preach your God to me today."

He was astounded. Was she really raising her voice to her own husband? Was she really blaspheming their Lord? Was Evelyn cursing their God? Had she lost her mind? He tried again, "Evelyn, dear, listen. God is still ... "

"Shut up, Patrick!" She was so loud and so forceful that she startled Ida and Estelle, Ned, and the Goodleafs. They all flinched, but remained where they were standing, silently motionless.

"You have known for 30 years that I have a twin," and pointing to Estelle, "that she was here with our little girl, and you kept that from me!"

"Twins?" Ned asked.

"Twins?" the Goodleafs also questioned.

Estelle blurted in astonishment to Rev. Harris, "Wait. You knew? You, you knew!?" And then pointing her finger at him (in that same jabbing motion that Evelyn did), "You knew I have a twin? You knew that Patty is my niece? And you said nothing? You allowed me to live alone all these years thinking I have no family while all along you knew?"

He did not respond.

Estelle's eyes turned dark red and swelled full just like her sister's. And she too lost her cool. She lunged toward him, trying to grab his throat with both her hands.

If she could have reached him, she would have strangled him. But she could not. Ned and Mr. Goodleaf threw themselves between Estelle and Rev. Harris and grabbed her to hold her back.

It was no easy feat as she was much stronger than she looked. Through her rage and tears, her arms and legs were thrashing. She desperately struggled to get loosed from them so she could squeeze the air out of him.

But they held on to her.

Rev. Harris attempted once more to take control of the situation, "If everyone would just settle down, God is my witness that ... "

"Wait", Ned cut him off this time. "I have waited for Patricia all these years because she would not marry me without your blessing. She would not move forward until you approved of me. And yet you have been deceiving her? Not me. You. And I have waited all these years for the approval of a liar?"

"Son, you do not understand," Rev. Harris was still trying to explain.

"I am not your son." And recalling how, until a few days ago, he was ordered to address Rev. Harris formally, he retorted, "My name is Jacob Nedfeather. I prefer that you call me 'Jacob' or 'Ned', but do not call me 'Son'."

The Goodleafs did not speak. Mrs. Goodleaf continued to stand motionless with her mouth dropped open, as if frozen solid. She was perplexed and wondering, *How on earth could he have done this to this beautiful family?*

Ida, who had suffered his indignance for decades, remembered how he called her names like, "Double D, the Wino". He would scorn her for not living a more Godly life. He would judge her and criticize her. He would insult her because she was unmarried and enjoying her many opportunities. She had only tolerated him because she loved Patty and Lewis so much. She finally moved from where they were all standing and stepped over to Evelyn. She wrapped her arms around her, and then looked to Rev. Harris in disgust (you know, that look like something smells rotten), "Shame on you."

He took a deep breath and then exhaled slowly, "God knows that I ... "

Evelyn, refusing to let him voice his rationalizations, had had enough. Still folded into Ida's embrace, she pointed to the front door when she commanded him, "Patrick, take your bags, take your excuses, take your sermons, take your God, and go."

Ida chimed in, "You heard her. Leave. Now. Before they turn Estelle loose on you."

4. GRIEF

Ralph had driven nonstop back into Manhattan from Shen Valley. On a typical road trip, he would have asked Rev. Harris if he needed to stop for refreshments or a restroom break. He did not this time because whenever he thought to and glanced the rearview mirror, he saw the exhausted man slumped over in deep sleep.

Ralph was much more than his driver. He was his confidante. He had served under his command in the Corps and retired shortly after Rev. Harris' retirement. When Ralph joined the church, he resumed the role of Rev. Harris' wingman and adjutant. He also became his private driver. Ralph had overheard conversations for decades and never betrayed their trust. He had learned his boss' habits to the point that he knew how to read his mood and when to arrange a night ride through the city to allow him to clear his head.

They had a bond of brotherhood. Ralph understood the burdens Rev. Harris bore all these years.

He respected him and his grace under the most difficult of circumstances. Interestingly, they never spoke of any of it. They did not communicate with words. Ralph would gesture with encouraging head nods, affirming eye contact in the rearview mirror, and heartening handshakes.

Ralph sympathized. In the past six days, his friend had reluctantly taken a trip that he was fearful might destroy his family, and it did.

Ralph witnessed Rev. Harris organizing a rescue mission for his daughter, who currently does not recognize him. She has forgotten him. She has no idea what her father just did for her. Ralph could not imagine a father moving heaven and earth for a child who does not even know to thank him. It is true that he kept a huge secret from her. Ralph wondered if this was punishment for that decision.

Ralph knew how much it hurt Rev. Harris to lose his only begotten son. And because their relationship had been strained, Rev. Harris only learned of his son's adoration of him posthumously. It was in death that love was made manifest.

Ralph also knew that Rev. Harris had just experienced his first argument (at least the first that any of them had witnessed) with his wife of almost 5 decades. She was understandably irate beyond description, but his intentions were good. He was in a difficult position and chose what he thought would be the most honorable action.

And after all that, in less than one week's time, Rev. Harris was returning home, alone, to sort it all out.

"Sir? Sir?" And then a little louder, "Sir?"

"Huh? Yes. What is it, Ralph?"

"There is the Skyline, Sir. We are home."

The Manhattan Skyline at night was therapeutic for Rev. Harris. It always had been. Whether from his penthouse apartment or from his chauffeured car as they rode along the Hudson River, the view was always stunning. He marveled at how the constructions are clustered together with staggering heights and spanning east to west to form a panoramic view. He admired their illumination and how their sprinkled lights form a rainbow of reflections in the water. That scene, back dropped against the night sky, would always draw his appreciation. It is a breathtaking sight.

Ralph pulled the car up for parking valet and opened the back door for Rev. Harris. When he recognized how tired his comrade appeared to be, Ralph signaled for the doorman's assistance.

The doorman called for a bellboy to retrieve his luggage and a security guard to escort Rev. Harris to his penthouse. The elongated lobby had marble flooring and the front desk resembled that of a hotel check-in. It expanded the full length of the lobby, from the front doors to the elevators. All four of its attendant stations were fully staffed. One of the attendants called upstairs to alert the Harrises' house manager, Phoebe, that Rev. Harris was on his way up to his penthouse.

Gold colored lights were built into the bottom of the counter to serve two purposes: they illuminated the walkway; and they accented the Oriental rug. The elegant antique brown rug was selected from the Nazmiyal Collection, customized for this foyer, and was valued at more than $1 million. The entire wall behind the attendants' station was a waterfall. The recess lights in the ceiling were tinted blue and aimed in the direction of the waterfall. The attendants always spoke softly, never louder than the sounds of the waterfall. At either end of the counter was an enormous flower arrangement, boasting colors of blue and gold. Rev. Harris usually appreciated the grandeur of the entrance, but not that night. His son had died. His daughter had forgotten him. His wife had disavowed him.

While the bellboy used a service elevator to take the luggage upstairs, the security guard assisted Rev. Harris down the long walk to the main elevators of the 34-story building. Ralph walked alongside them. They would use the private elevator that was designated exclusively for the four penthouse residences so, thankfully, they would not have to wait very long.

Phoebe was waiting to receive Rev. Harris. She was unassuming in appearance: not tall, not much makeup, a remarkably short haircut, modest jewelry, a basic black dress, and low-heeled black shoes.

Her name suited her perfectly. Her parents had named her after Phoebe, the first-century Christian woman mentioned by the Apostle Paul in his Epistle to the

Romans. Paul refers to her both as a deacon and as a helper or patron of many. The biblical Phoebe was a woman of some means who was generous with her support of others. The same could be said for the Phoebe who managed the Harrises' household. She had a specific leadership role in their lives.

She wore a large headset similar to those worn by sports announcers, and she carried a mobile tablet. Thanks to communications she received from Ralph while they drove, she had already alerted the condominium staff of various concerns. This professional group attends to all the owners. Each owner has a house manager who coordinates the services for their home. Where the Harrises were concerned, that would be Phoebe.

She had contacted all the necessary staff to address matters of distress. The nurse would come and check Rev. Harris' vital signs and assess his physical condition. If she deemed it necessary, she would call in his physician. The chef would prepare him a light meal. The nurse would suggest a menu based on his physical condition. The housekeeper would unpack his luggage and, under normal circumstances, draw a bath for Mrs. Harris, but tonight he would just start the shower for Rev. Harris. The penthouse custodian would light a wood-burning fire in their parlor fireplace. The crackling sound and lumber smell would be soothing. His executive assistant at the church would share with both Phoebe and Ralph a copy of his itinerary for the following day.

Phoebe, confident that she had covered all the bases, was standing at the elevator when they arrived. She did not anticipate what followed.

"Good evening, Sir. Welcome home."

He nodded in acknowledgement but did not speak.

Concerned with his faint appearance, she continued. "Sir, please come with me to the parlor. I have arranged for a few services."

He nodded again. He was barely to the door when his legs buckled and gave out beneath him. Ralph and the security guard caught him. On either side of him, they threw one of his arms over their shoulders and helped him walk over to the parlor.

The original building design was for 34 stories; however, the 33rd and 34th floors had been combined to accommodate the 4 most prestigious condominiums. The Harrises and the other 3 owners each had a 2-story dwelling, each consuming a full corner of the building. The Harrises, of course, had the better corner with the best view.

Escorted to his parlor in silence, the only sounds were Phoebe's low heels on the Westhollow hardwood floors. The solid wood flooring is heavy and more resilient than engineered floor panels. The Harrises had it upgraded to an exotic wood before they moved in, a Brazilian cherry. They are beautiful floors and for most people they are prohibitively expensive; however, Evelyn liked them, so Rev. Harris obliged.

The Oriental rug in the middle of the floor was from the same Nazmiyal Collection as the rug in the foyer. It was white with very faint tan marks that looked like streaks. Centered on the rug was a white marble coffee table on a tan stand. Surrounding the rug were two extended-length tan sofas, each built to seat 4-5 people at a time, and two leather armchairs. All had white throw pillows.

There were no walls in the 2-story parlor. There were windows. They spanned 24 feet from ceiling to floor and exposed the city skyline. Each window was framed with custom draperies that added a pop of color, a tiny tan and white paisley print, and they were never drawn closed.

Ralph, Phoebe, and the security guard helped Rev. Harris to the seat closest to the fireplace. He glanced over at the stairs realizing that he was far too weak to climb them. It was a glass stairway with wooden steps that matched the floors. He would have to walk up 12 steps to the landing, turn and walk up another 12 steps. That was undoubtedly out of the realm of current possibilities.

Abandoning his statuesque posture that they had come to know of him, he slumped over in the chair. Ralph asked Phoebe and the security guard if he could have a moment alone with the Reverend. They obliged and retreated to the penthouse office.

Ralph whispered, "Sir, are you okay?"

Rev. Harris did not respond.

"Sir, I am concerned. Are you okay, Sir?"

He looked up and exposed something Ralph had never seen. In more than 25 years of working with him, Ralph had never seen Rev. Harris emotional. Not once.

At a loss for words, Ralph gently laid one hand on his shoulder. He felt him quiver.

His eyes filled.

Ralph removed his eyeglasses from his face and kneeled beside him. "I know, Sir. I know." Ralph's eyes filled as well.

Using the remote control device beside the chair, Ralph signaled for Phoebe.

He could hear her cute little footsteps quickly approaching. That always made him smile.

Ralph issued the directive, "Phoebe, after the nurse checks him and he eats, I will help him upstairs. I will stay in one of the guest rooms tonight."

Phoebe noticed that neither Rev. Harris nor Ralph looked up at her. "Very well, Ralph. And I will contact his assistant at the church to cancel his appointments for tomorrow."

On any other day, Rev. Harris would have opposed to having someone plan for him. That night, he just did not have the energy to contest.

When he was finally ready to retire for the evening, Phoebe signaled for the housekeeper who quietly entered the parlor. He announced that the shower was ready. What that means is the water was the exact temperature that Rev. Harris prefers, and the same could be said for the fresh towels in the warmer. His purple silk pajamas with matching bathrobe and slippers had been placed near the shower.

The housekeeper offered to help Rev. Harris up the stairs but Ralph and Phoebe, protecting his pride, simultaneously declined his offer.

"Let's head upstairs, Sir", Ralph suggested and offered a firm hand to help him out of the chair.

Rev. Harris walked with assistance, perhaps slightly stronger now that he had eaten and hydrated. Ralph still walked closely by his side.

Finally, upstairs and at the end of the hallway, they reached the king suite. In all these years, Ralph had never seen the Harrises' chambers. It was regal. Remarkably regal. It was unlike anything Ralph had ever seen.

The flooring was, of course, of the same Brazilian cherry wood as the lower level of the apartment. And the rug completed the collection of the Oriental rugs. He would have expected that.

The ceiling, well, he needed more time to take in the spectacular architectural design. There were several layers of white molding with a floral pattern. The molding outlined the borders of all four lavender colored walls. Inside the molding there was a mural of a purple field. It covered the ceiling. The flowers were winter annuals called Henbit and Purple Deadnettle. Both are in the mint family. They grow in fields every year, but they are especially colorful in years with mild winters. In addition to those painted on the ceiling, live floras were in pots that hang from each corner of the room and were mixed with lavender plants. Together they produced a wonderful fragrance of mint and lavender, and lots of natural purple.

In the center of the mural was a circle of floral molding and within that circle were purple silk drapes woven into a ring pattern. Outside the circle more of the same drapes hang into a soft, flowing design that made a romantic and dreamy enclosure around the bed. The round bed was in the center of the floor, embellished in purple, gold, and white.

Ralph was still taking in the splendor of the majestic room when Phoebe interrupted his awestruck state, "Ralph?"

"Yes. I am sorry." And gesturing to one of the purple upholstered chairs against the wall, "Please, Sir. Have a seat."

Just as he sat, the housekeeper offered to help Rev. Harris to the shower. Phoebe suggested that she and Ralph give him privacy.

Ralph agreed.

When he was finished with his shower and his bedding was turned down, he gestured for the housekeeper to leave him. The room felt large and empty. For the first time, he would be sleeping in that bed without his wife. Climbing into his side of the bed, he stretched forth his arm to where she would rest. The linen was cold.

He replayed the events of the week in his mind: agreeing to take the trip, searching for Patty, losing

Lewis, and then hurting Evelyn. The grief overtook him, and tears began to stream down his cheeks. He opened his mouth to cry but nothing came out. There was no sound. It felt as if he was choking on his cry. He burst into a sweat. His chest tightened. He thought he might be yelling but there was in fact no sound.

At that very moment, Ralph was in a guest room at the other end of the hall and, although the penthouse was completely noiseless, he sensed urgency. Something alarmed Ralph. Simultaneously, something distressing aroused inside Phoebe. They each ran from their rooms back to the king suite.

Rev. Harris was curled into a fetal position and sweating and crying and his mouth was open, but he did not make a sound. His weeping was inaudible. Phoebe and Ralph both climbed up into his bed and hugged the Reverend. When they enfolded him and held on tightly to him, then the sound released.

It was loud. It was mighty. It echoed throughout the penthouse, "Eli, Eli, Lama Sabachthani?"

5. Palm Springs

Ida arrived at Palm Springs International Airport at 6:14 PM on Monday, as ordered by the General. Her meeting was scheduled for the following day at 29 Palms Marine Corp Base. While the base commissary and exchange could meet all of her travel needs, her hosts considered the stressful week she had just endured and made more pleasing accommodations for her. They had not bothered to share the details with her just yet. She only knew when to board the plane and to look for Major Paul Cory when she landed.

She was relaxed. The bottomless wine service on the plane helped with that.

She descended the escalators and caught a glimpse of herself in a mirror. She wore a wine-colored Hermès dress. It was 100% silk made of Moroccan crepe. The sleeves stopped just at her elbows. It had a high-waisted built-in belt, and combined with the plunging V-neck, it was incredibly flattering. Below the tie belt, there was ample fabric. If she sat and spread the dress out, the silk would stretch to her fingertips' reach. When she stood, it was an elegant flow of drapery that reached down to her calves. She would not normally have worn such a lavish dress on an airplane but, again, she had no idea what to expect upon landing and she always liked to make a memorable first impression.

At the bottom of the escalators, there were many greeters holding signs and mobile devices with names on them. Some donned black suits, a few were wearing civilian clothing, and others were in military uniforms. To her far left, she spotted a gentleman holding an iPad that read, "Ms. Ida Wilson".

She smiled and waved at him.

He recognized her from the media coverage of Patty's extraction the prior week and from the intel his office had gathered. Somehow, she was even more attractive in person. But he was a professional, on duty, and he did not smile.

"Ms. Wilson?"

"Yes. Hello."

"Good evening, Ma'am. Welcome to Palm Springs. I am Major Cory."

He was taller than average. Despite her wearing heels, she still had to look upward to make eye contact. "It is nice to meet you."

"You as well, Ma'am. Your luggage is being retrieved and will be taken to our car. I'd be honored to ride with you and escort you to your resort."

"That'll be nice. Thank you."

He was wearing a Service A uniform, which comprises forest green trousers and a matching coat, and with 10 rows of ribbons and badges on the left side of his chest. She didn't know what they represented but it looked impressive. He had a huge, red insignia that had a star in the middle on his left arm. His shirt and tie were a matching desert sand color. His appearance was pristine, almost sterile. His hair was cut extremely close, barely existing, and his face was clean-shaven. His appearance was hardened with tough skin, serious eyes, and pursed lips that did not curl upward. Perhaps a smile would have softened him.

The ride to the resort was quiet. Major Cory was not much of a conversationalist. He looked intently straight ahead. Ida looked out the window at the desert and mountain views. The resort city appeared to have been designed for tourists with more than 130 hotels, resorts, and bed and breakfasts, each surrounded by restaurants and dining spots. She was welcoming the rest and relaxation that the city presented.

Ida reflected on the events of the previous 10 days:

On Friday, she had driven from her home in Manhattan to Shen Valley for Patty's retirement party.

Saturday and Sunday, she had participated in the search and rescue.

Also, on Sunday she had waited with the family to receive the news of Patty's surgeries and learned of Lewis' demise.

On Monday, Patty awakened, and the phone call came from Major Cory.

Following Patty's post-surgical tests came the sad news of her condition, and then Ida witnessed the disheartening episode of Mr. and Mrs. Harris.

She then had a mere four days to help Evelyn and Estelle plan to ambulate Patty from the hospital to a rehabilitation facility, plan Lewis' funeral, and prepare for her trip to the west coast.

With another challenging week ahead, she would have her initial meeting on Monday, follow up meetings on Tuesday, fly back to New York on Wednesday, and assist the Harrises on Thursday and Friday in preparation for Lewis' very public funeral at their mega church on Saturday.

She was exhausted. She was sad. She was alone.

Out of pure habit, she reached for her phone to text Patty. That is what she always did when she needed her friend. When she realized that not only was Patty incapacitated but that she had also forgotten their decades of friendship, Ida felt sick in her stomach. She assured herself that all would be well once she showed pictures and videos to Patty to trigger recollections. They would have to reminisce to generate recalls. It would be fine, she hoped. Patty would pull through, she prayed.

And then there was Lewis' passing away. He knew that Ida loved him as a sister loves her brother. He knew that she was in his corner always. He never doubted that. But he was gone. Forever. Lewis was gone.

There were also the mixed emotions of Mrs. Harris' bittersweet discovery. She learned that she has a twin and that is amazing. She also learned that her husband has known all these years and never told her. Ida could not imagine how that kind of betrayal must hurt.

It was all too much to digest. Tears began trickling down her face.

She wished the stone cold, expressionless man in the starchily creased uniform who was riding next to her could offer some consolation. Could he inquire about her state of mind? Could he do anything to help her at that moment? Could he offer her a handkerchief at least? She wiped her face with tissue from her purse, and with a slightly shaky voice and sniffling nose asked, "How much further?"

Still looking forward, "Just a few more minutes, Ma'am."

Maybe he's made of steel, she thought.

Finally arriving, she marveled at the sweeping views of golf fairways set against the timeless backdrop of the Palm Desert mountainside. Upon entering the grounds, she noticed almost two acres of family-friendly features, including two 100-foot waterslides ringed by a 425-foot lazy river. That would be great for kids, but she was hoping for something more restful.

Thankfully, her hosts had planned for such tranquility. Just a few buildings back, she checked in and entered her suite. Ida was immediately greeted with the serenity of a surprising water view in the desert. French doors opened to a cozy bedroom with plentiful closet space. The impeccably renovated bathroom featured travertine tile and a rolling door. The sprawling patio revealed stunning lake, mountain, and garden views.

"This is exactly what I need," she said to Major Cory.

"We trust you will enjoy your stay, Ma'am."

So formal, she thought. But she really wanted companionship, so she asked, "Do you have any plans this evening?"

"I need to run a quick errand, Ma'am."

"Of course. I see."

"Did you have something in mind?" He was hoping.

"A dinner companion would be nice."

He didn't need time to think about it. "I can come back. How's 2000hrs?"

She looked as if she were calculating.

"That is 8 o'clock PM, Ma'am.

She really wished he would stop the 'Ma'am' thing, but she desperately desired company, so she would deal with it. "Oh. Yes. If it is not too much to ask, sure. Where will we go? What is the attire?"

Looking her up and down as if judging her outfit, he replied, "Ma'am, please wear that dress, those shoes, and that fragrance. Please do not change a thing."

It was a compliment indeed. Still, however, there was nothing expressive from him. No smiles. No embrace.

No warmth. Did he realize what she was going through? Was he even human?

Ida responded politely, "Thank you. See you soon."

With a quick and formal pivot, he turned and exited her suite.

She only needed a few minutes to freshen up since she did not have to change her clothes. That left time for a little relaxation. She was sitting out on the patio enjoying the view when her phone rang. He was punctual. He had been gone just over an hour and he was calling from the lobby at 7:50 PM.

"What are you doing?" he asked.

"Marveling."

"At what?"

"At the view from my patio and the stately mountains reflecting off the lake. It is majestic. I imagine it is similar to the glory in the heavens. There is nothing like this in Manhattan.

The man of steel had no response other than, "I am in the lobby." It was almost as if he were rushing her.

She understood. "I will be right there."

Ida had been perusing dinner menus from the various resort restaurants. Some were casual. One was formal. She correctly guessed which one he had chosen. Yes, of course he had selected the one formal dining option. And if that's not enough, he attempted to plan their evening.

He proudly announced, "I made reservations for 9:00 PM. I thought we could enjoy the lounge until then. Is that okay with you?"

"Sure," was a gracious response but she could not imagine just hanging out with him for a whole hour before dinner. And she was hungry.

"Great. Come down the hall on your left, all the way to the back. I am at the bar."

"Okay. See you shortly." Their call ended.

She became hopeful. *The bar. That is encouraging. That means wine. I hope it's the good stuff, and lots of it.*

When she arrived in the lounge, she did not see the green and tan uniform. It was odd because he had just called her from there. Slightly annoyed, she took small, slow steps, trying to spot him.

He saw her looking for him and was amused. He was off duty now and had changed out of his uniform. He was also hiding behind the large vase with the dozen roses he had delivered for her.

She texted him, "I do not see you."

He replied to her, "I see you. Keep walking. You're getting close."

Approaching the end of the bar there was only one person. He turned to her, wearing a white Gianni Versace, loose fit denim shirt, and the matching white jeans. His biceps were bulging through the sleeves. The jeans were slightly baggy and ripped at the knees. All that white against his dark chocolate skin was remarkable. He stood to greet her, and she noticed that he wore Timberland boots. They were also white, suede, and unlaced. He was casual. And styled. And handsome.

He reached out to her, "Hello Beautiful."

"Well, hello, Stranger."

"I took the liberty of ordering appetizers, your favorites: spicy nachos, crab cake bites, and spinach dip."

"You've done some research."

"Yes, I have. And your favorite wine, a Cabernet Sauvignon." He began to pour from the chilling bottle, "It is not from Shenandoah Valley though. I am afraid the best I could do was a local vineyard in Napa Valley."

His sarcasm was duly noted. When he turned the bottle to show her the label, she saw that it was a Vine Cliff Winery Napa Valley Cabernet Sauvignon 2014 (SRP $135). It opened up with aromas of cassis, black cherry, and hints of mint.

"Excellent choice! You, Sir, selected well," and she held up her glass to clink his.

"I'm glad you approve. I'll have our second bottle sent to your suite for us to enjoy after our dinner."

She smiled and sipped.

He smiled, finally.

6. REHABILITATION

Patty would be transferring from the hospital to the rehabilitation facility today. She would have a long road to recovery but at least this facility was local. She would be surrounded by friends who loved her.

Estelle and Evelyn, with Ida's and Ned's assistance, had screened them virtually but, because they were also planning Lewis' funeral in New York, this would be the first opportunity to tour it and meet the staff in person. None of them were excited about this part but they knew the sooner Patty began a rehab program, the better her chances of recovery.

They had all driven together: Estelle, Evelyn, Ned, and the Case Manager from the hospital. Together they would review her treatment plan, see her room and meet her roommate, and sit with her doctor to ask any medically related questions. It was nice having the Case Manager with them because she served as a liaison between the hospital and the rehabilitation center. Just as she had coordinated the meeting with the surgical team, she had also managed all communications with the rehab team. She had spared the family many of the details.

The Case Manager's contact at the rehab was their Facility Manager. She guided their tour.

"This is the Orthopedic Therapy Center", she explained. "We'll start here with your tour."

The room was large, and its layout resembled commercial fitness centers. There were high ceilings with fluorescent lights and several different areas of equipment. In the front just as they entered that room, were two parallel bars, arms-length apart. "Here's where Patty will learn to stand again and take small steps. Her routine may be similar to the gentleman you see here."

There was a man standing between the bars and a therapist stood close by outside the bars. She was supporting him by holding a band that was secured around his waist. In front of him were three small steps. It was obvious that he was learning to walk up and down steps again. He was smiling proudly, and his therapist was encouraging him as he ascended and then descended the three steps. Evidently, he had reached a huge milestone in his recovery process. Patty's family was encouraged by the demonstration.

To the immediate left was an office behind a glass wall. The Facility Manager signaled to the personnel in the office and then spoke again, "Let's go meet Patty's team."

There were 12 people, all dressed in dark gray scrub suits, smiling at the family. They were a diverse group with varying ethnicities and differing ages, and they were friendly. They all pleasantly greeted at the same time and one of them said, "Welcome to our family."

Simultaneously, Evelyn and Estelle exhaled. The thought of Patty being among "family" was reassuring for them. They knew she would be in good company.

The Case Manager was marking off boxes on a checklist and then nodded to the Facility Manager, apparently, that they could move on. The coordination of the tour had obviously been well planned.

"Each person in this room will have a role in Patty's recovery. Over the next several weeks, you will meet with them individually to discuss her progress. For now, let's continue your tour."

They walked past the patient who was walking between the parallel bars when he called out to them. "Excuse me?"

"Yes, Sir?" the Facility Manager answered.

"Tomorrow, I will begin to use a walker and eventually a cane. Patty will do the same. I am sure of it."

The Case Manager asked, "How do you know Patty?"

"I do not know her personally. I saw her story on the news." And, then looking directly at Ned, "I recognize you from the TV. Good job, young man!"

Ned merely nodded. He was still taking it all in and had not spoken much since seeing Patty in the hospital a few days earlier.

There must have been a dozen different stations where staff worked with patients. It would just be a matter of time before Patty would be among them.

The next room was a huge swimming pool filled with warm water. It also contained a variety of equipment: floatation devices, tubes, slides, boards, and ropes.

The next room looked like a model of a small studio apartment. There was a kitchen area, a working bathroom, and a bed. "This is where Patty will eventually regain her independence. She will relearn cooking, personal care, and all the skills necessary for a self-regulating home life."

This was a lot to process. The realization of how hard she would have to work and how long her progress could take, was disconcerting for all of them.

They walked down a corridor of doctors' offices. Each had their name and department labeled outside their door. There was also a laboratory and several examination rooms on that same hallway.

Continuing the tour, they came upon a room with people sitting in folding chairs in a circle. The tour did not interrupt the group therapy and there was no explanation necessary of what was occurring there. Clearly, Patty would have emotional support on her recovery journey.

"The final stop before meeting with her doctor is Patty's room. You can meet her roommate and see her living quarters."

When they approached the room, the Case Manager nodded in approval to the Facility Manager. The room, as requested, had a view of the mountains. If anything would soothe and inspire Patty, it would be those spectacular views.

Her roommate, Jillian, was in bed reading and looked up when the family entered. Ned recognized her.

"Jillian?"

"Hi, Ned."

"What happened? How are you?"

"I was on a back road when the earthquake occurred. A tree fell over on my car and both my legs were crushed."

"Oh my God. I am so sorry."

"Thanks. But it could be worse. I am in the best rehab program in the area. I count that a blessing."

"Please pardon my manners," he continued and then gestured to Evelyn and Estelle. "This is Patty's mother, Mrs. Harris, and you already know Estelle."

"Pleased to meet you, Ma'am," she said to Evelyn.

Evelyn was unsettled by how little she knew of Patty's friends. And what disturbed her most about it, was that it was because of lies. Her father and her husband conspired to keep her truth a secret and because of them she has missed out on 20 years of her daughter's life.

Estelle moved closer to hug her, "I am glad you will be okay." Then Estelle explained to Evelyn, "Jillian is the track coach at the college. She and Patty are good friends."

Jillian added, "and we sometimes run together."

Evelyn nodded, "I am glad you survived, and I pray for your full recovery."

"Thank you. Patty and I will race again someday. I am sure of if it."

The Case Manager added, "And it's good that the two of you will rehabilitate together. You can encourage one another. It would be much more difficult alone."

The Facility Manager wrapped up the introductions, "Jillian, we will leave you to your reading and see you again soon, once Patty is settled in."

"How long before she comes?"

"She's en route now, so momentarily."

"Okay. I cannot wait to see her.

They exited the room and were led to another wing where there was a waiting area. After nearly an hour of walking and meeting, they welcomed the break. The room was newly decorated in neutral colors of taupe, gray, and cream. The track lighting softened the atmosphere. The modern art, contemporary furniture, and plush carpeting made for an inviting space.

"Feel free to wait here for Dr. Ian Ellis." Then, pointing to an area across the room, "There are refreshments for you to enjoy: coffee, tea, water, and snacks. After you have met with Dr. Ellis, I will come back."

After about 15 minutes, they were relaxing and beginning to refresh when he entered the room.

He must have been close to Evelyn's age. He was strikingly handsome, almost distractingly so. He was 6'2" and slender. His haircut was so precise that he must have left a barber just moments prior. There were 2 or 3 slight wrinkles on his forehead, and not those that imply age but, rather, sophistication. How's that possible? His eyebrows were so thick and full that that they overshadowed his eyes. His immaculately trimmed mustache and beard were sprinkled with gray and silver strands.

He was beginning to introduce himself when his prominent British accent manifested. "Good morning. I am Dr. Ellis. I am a specialist in post-traumatic amnesia.

"Good morning," they all sang out in unison.

He continued, "I was educated in London. I came to the U.S. to further my research, fell in love with the area, and decided to make it home."

They each introduced themselves:

"I am Evelyn Harris, Patricia's mother."

"I am Estelle, her aunt."

"I am the hospital Case Manager and liaison between this facility and the hospital."

"...and I am Ned, Patty's fiancé."

"I see. And, I was expecting to also meet her father, Rev. Harris."

"He will not be here," Evelyn responded tersely.

Her response was perplexing. He had witnessed the mission on television and could see the father's love for his daughter. It was surprising that Rev. Harris was not there. He continued, "I see. I have read Patty's case thoroughly. I also followed your family's tragedy on the news. My condolences. I am sorry for your loss."

Respectfully, this was the first time that day that anyone had mentioned Lewis.

Evelyn stared off into space with that deer caught in the headlights look.

"I am so sorry for your loss, Ma'am."

His repetition brought her back, "Thank you."

He had a checklist identical to Marcy's and he methodically reviewed the plan with the family. He discussed the outcomes of Patty's surgeries, protocols to prevent a slip or fall, her daily routine, her weekly schedule, their state-of-the-art assistive devices like electronic walkers, group therapy options, and a variety of rehab services.

The family was confident that Patty was in the best facility available. Dr. Ellis was finishing up when he received a text message. "Ah, I see that Patty is settled in her room. If you have questions for me, I am available to you. Here's my card," and when handing it to Evelyn, "Please feel free to call me at any time."

He then texted the Facility Manager: "All done here. Family is waiting for you."

She returned to the family waiting area. "I realize it is a lot to take in, but please remember that we are all here to support you as well as Patty. We are honored to be here for you." She paused for a minute. "If you are ready to see Patty now, I will escort you to her room."

They all stood immediately and followed her along the maze of corridors.

Patty's appearance was a little easier for them to digest this time. Her legs were still casted, both her hands were bandaged, and her head was completely wrapped in medical gauze, but it was no longer in a stabilizer. Also, now, there were no tubes in her throat, nose, and arms.

The Case Manager spoke first. "Patty, I am your Case Manager from the hospital, the liaison here at the rehab, and just so you know, you are my son's favorite professor."

Patty smiled.

Then, pointing to her roommate, "and this is Jillian. She is the track coach at the college where you work. She will fill you in more a little later."

Jillian nodded in assurance.

The Case Manager continued, "This is part of your family. I will let them introduce themselves."

Evelyn and Ned each took a turn, keeping their introductions brief. They had been instructed to do so because she was still heavily sedated and likely tired from the transport.

Evelyn gently touched her hand. "I am your mother, Patricia. They will provide a writing pad for you once the bandages are off your hands and we will be able to communicate. I will be here with you every step of the way."

Patty nodded with appreciation and she thought of the mama dear and her loving care of the feeble fawn.

7. MATTIE

When Phoebe called the church regarding Rev. Harris' work itinerary, she was informed that his Executive Assistant was on short-term leave and that a temporary assistant, Mattie, would be filling in for her.

"Hello, this is Mattie."

"Hi, Mattie. My name is Phoebe. I am the House Manager for Rev. and Mrs. Harris. How are you?"

"I am well, thank you. What can I do for you?"

"Rev. Harris has returned from Virginia but I suggest that we clear his calendar for a couple of days of rest. Could you assist me with that?"

"Sure. I can do that, and I am working with the associate clergy to finalize the plans for Lewis' funeral service. I will be reaching out to Mrs. Harris shortly for her approval.

"Excellent. Thank you."

"Oh, Phoebe, one more thing…"

"Yes?"

"There are documents that require his signature. I can bring them over to the penthouse."

"That would be fine. Call me when the documents are ready, and we can set up a time that works for Rev. Harris."

Shortly afterward, Mattie called Evelyn.

"Hello. This is Evelyn Harris."

In a flat and casual tone, "Hi, I am Mattie. I'm your husband's temporary EA."

"I beg your pardon."

"Rev. Harris' temporary EA, Executive Assistant. The other girl is on personal leave or something."

"I see. What can I do for you?"

"I'm sorry for your loss. I'm helping to finalize the details of your son's funeral service. Did you receive an email?"

"Yes, I did."

"Do you approve the details?"

"Yes, they are all fine. Thank you."

"Cool. I will have your husband sign the papers."

"Reverend Harris."

"Excuse me?"

"*Reverend Harris* is the proper way to refer to him. That is his title in the church, not *my husband*."

"Oh. Okay. I will have Rev. Harris sign the papers. And, if you need anything please let me know."

"I will."

"Okay, I will see you at the funeral on Saturday. Bye."

Mattie called Phoebe back.

"Hello, this is Phoebe."

"Hey Phoebe, it's Mattie."

"Hello Mattie."

"The documents are ready for your boss' signature."

"Reverend Harris."

"Okay, the documents are ready for Rev. Harris' signature."

Something about Mattie did not set well with Phoebe. "Mattie, could you send them electronically? He is still resting, and it would save you a trip uptown."

"I need hard copies because I have to drop off originals at the insurance company and the funeral home. I can be there in an hour."

"Understood. Please call when you reach the lobby. I will have security escort you up to the penthouse."

"No problem. See you soon."

Phoebe, as unimpressed with Mattie's mannerisms as Evelyn, also chose to ignore them. There were much more pressing issues to address than an unpolished temporary EA, or so she thought.

As instructed, when Mattie arrived, she called Phoebe. "I'm downstairs. I'm getting out the car now."

"Check in at the front desk in the lobby and wait for security to bring you up."

"I don't need all that. I can just come up."

"The visitors' policy states otherwise. Please sign in and wait for an escort."

When Mattie saw the lobby with the long desk, floral arrangements, custom rug, and waterfall, she took out her cellphone and began taking selfies. A security guard quickly ran over to her to inform her that photos were not permitted. After he watched her delete all 12 of them from her phone he escorted her to the private elevator, where his card was required to select the penthouse level.

Phoebe, in her uniform attire, the modest black dress and low-heeled black pumps, was astonished when she saw Mattie.

Mattie, 5'10" and mostly legs, looked, unfortunately, liked she sounded. Beneath more than enough makeup was probably a beautiful face, but the exaggerated eyebrows, spider-like fake lashes, sparkling green eyeshadow, and mounds of foundation concealed any hint of natural beauty. Her hair had been smoothly pulled up into what could have been a very neat ponytail, but the extension that obviously clipped on detracted from the style. The color and texture of the clip-on did not match her natural hair, and it hung all the way down to her waist.

At first glance, it appeared she was wearing a short, green sweater dress. Upon closer examination though, Phoebe realized it was a sweater, not a dress. That explained why it stopped just beneath her buttocks. Speaking of backsides, hers appeared unusually large and misshaped, lumpy.

And then at the bottom of her mile-long legs were her shoes. She wore platform strappy stilettos, at least 4", metallic gold. They must have been a little uncomfortable because she walked as if her feet hurt, almost limping.

"Hey Phoebe. I am Mattie."

"Hello, Mattie. Welcome."

She entered the penthouse speaking loudly. "Girl, this place is off the chain! Do you get to live here?"

Ignoring her comment and question, "My office is right here. Please have a seat. May I see the documents?"

"Yeah, sure. Here ya go."

Phoebe carefully read each of the documents, a total of 12 pages. She then informed Mattie that she would have them signed and scan a copy for the Harrises' personal files. Mattie should wait in Phoebe's office until she returned.

The temptation was too great for Mattie. She began to wander around, taking in the beauty of the views, the décor, and the sheer ambiance of the penthouse. She would have taken a few photos for her social media, but she recalled the little episode in the lobby, so she thought it best not to. When Phoebe returned and saw her walking to toward the parlor, she walked up to her quickly.

"Please, Ma'am. We should keep your visit to my office."

Ignoring the polite request, "This is amazing. I have never seen anything like this."

"We should return to my office now, please."

"Okay. Fine."

Phoebe worked quickly to make the copies and only had one request from Rev. Harris.

"Mattie, Rev. Harris would like to have a private viewing of Lewis on Friday."

"But the public viewing is on Saturday, one hour before the service begins."

"Yes. I am aware. He would like a private moment with his son Friday evening, at 6:00 PM. Please arrange it with the funeral home."

"I understand."

With all those matters addressed, Phoebe called for the security guard to come escort Mattie back down the elevator and out of the building.

Mattie was back in her Uber wondering how long Mrs. Harris would be in Virginia. She knew she would be coming to Manhattan for the funeral on Saturday but would likely return to Shen Valley to be with Patty.

The following morning, she reported to the church office early and called Evelyn.

"Good morning, this is Evelyn Harris."

"Good morning, Mrs. Harris. This is Mattie."

"Hello Mattie."

"Hi. I am following up because the arrangements are final for Saturday. The public viewing will be one hour before the service starts. The service will be closed-casket."

"Okay."

"And, umm, should we expect you on Friday?"

"I plan to arrive Saturday morning, as we already discussed. I am coming directly to the church."

"Yes, Ma'am. Your husband is having a private viewing, just him, on Friday, and I didn't know if you were now planning to be there as well."

Gently correcting her again, "*Rev. Harris* obviously wants that time alone with Lewis. I will respect that."

"Yes, Ma'am. Well, I will see you Saturday."

"You will. Goodbye, Mattie."

"Bye."

This was all good news for Mattie. As suspected, Rev. Harris would be home alone for the next few days. And he would view his son's remains alone Friday evening. And after the funeral on Saturday, he would return to his penthouse alone to grieve.

Mattie began to brainstorm ways to console him because, *it is not good for man to be alone.*

8. LEWIS' FUNERAL

The funeral home had arranged for Rev. Harris' private time with Lewis as he had requested. His viewing was not at the funeral home. It was at the church.

The casket was opened, with an embalmed Lewis lying in rest. Surrounding his casket were countless flower arrangements. So many, that it looked like he was resting amid a garden.

But not just any garden, perhaps Keukenhof, also known as the Garden of Europe. That is one of the world's largest flower gardens, situated in the town of Lisse, in the Netherlands. Keukenhof Park covers an area of 79 acres and approximately 7 million flower bulbs are planted in the gardens annually. That is what the church resembled on the eve before they would bid farewell to Lewis.

New Life Kingdom Church of Christ in Manhattan ("NLKCCM") is a megachurch with one of the largest congregations in the United States. It averages about

60,000 attendees per week. The 17,000-seat stadium is home to six services on Sundays: four English-language services, and two Spanish-language services. It also houses a Wednesday noon-day service, mostly geared toward the elderly.

It was formerly the Ramses II Stadium, and is prominently located in the Inwood neighborhood at the northern tip of the island of Manhattan, New York City. It was acquired by NLKCCM shortly after Rev. Harris became the pastor. His first major fundraiser was to cover the expenses for adding a dome, enclosing the arena. He accomplished that by preserving the track and field, and when church is not in service, leasing out the stadium for various sports events.

That had always been a sore subject for Patty. Her father purchased an Olympic track and field, preserved it for people from all over the world to compete on it, and yet he forbade her to do so. One of the reasons she desperately wanted to escape New York was to leave that constant reminder behind her.

After the space surrounding Lewis was completely filled with flowers, the remaining arrangements were placed all the way around the 400-meter track. That is 400m (.25 miles) in Lane 1, and it is an 8-lane track. All the lanes had flowers spread throughout. There were tulips, hyacinths, daffodils, lilies, roses, carnations, and irises. The flower deliveries had been arriving in truck loads non-stop for a week.

That Friday evening Rev. Harris had come to the garden alone to have a final visit with his son. He stood over him. He prayed for him. He talked to him. Those precious moments would remain with Rev. Harris forever.

On Saturday, it was not surprising that by the time Lewis' public viewing began, the arena was filled to capacity. His photo journal had gone viral. He was famous. All seats in the stadium were occupied and there were no bad seats because of the jumbotrons at either end zone.

Those who did not arrive early enough to acquire a seat inside gathered around the additional jumbotrons outside. There were two of them, one on either side of the building. They were similar to the one used at Cowboys Stadium, which currently boasts the largest jumbotron in the NFL. It is a beast of an LED measuring 160 feet wide and 72 feet tall. The Cowboys have one. NLKCCM has four of them.

For those who were not fortunate enough to make it out to the in-person service there was, of course, live streaming on the Internet and local television networks. As many who had watched via the media when Lewis photographed his sister's rescue mission, were now tuned in to bid him farewell. It seemed that the entire country mourned the loss of Patrick 'Lewis' Harris, Jr.

When the viewing began, the camera crew scanned the arena, showing footage of the massive crowd.

It was reverently quiet. The stadium was filled with sorrowful soundlessness. Both inside the arena and outside weighed the heavy hearts of a silent crowd for the entire hour of the viewing.

Rev. and Mrs. Harris had agreed upon and approved all the details of the service. Well, at least he thought they had. There must have been some misunderstandings. He had approved the hymns to be sung and insisted that, according to Church of Christ tradition, musical instruments would not be used. He was also adamant that a minister, a Man of God, read from the Bible and directed the congregation throughout the service.

Evelyn had other ideas. The family was lining up just outside his church office for the processional when, to his surprise, music began playing throughout the stadium. Music. Live music. With instruments.

Big band music began to play in center field. Not just a big band though. Oh no, there were three 13-piece bands on the field. They were playing Lewis' anthem song.

Rev. Harris looked at Evelyn in disgust, "What have you done?"

"It is called *music*."

"What are they playing? It is not a hymn that I recognize?"

"It is not a hymn."

"What is it?"

"It is our son's favorite song. You'll have the lyrics shortly. I had them printed on the back of the Program."

Just then a timid gentleman wearing white gloves distributed Funeral Programs to everyone in line. He knew Rev. Harris would not be pleased. Shying away from eye contact, he indicated that they were ready to proceed into the stadium. On the back of the Program, the lyrics were indeed printed. For everyone else the lyrics scrolled on the jumbotrons.

The processional began with Rev. Harris, Evelyn, and GG leading a line of 66 family members, friends, church clergy, and close colleagues. They also included Lewis' photography friends, work partners, and college buddies.

Just as they entered the arena, remarkably, the crowd began to sing in unison, along with the big bands. No one encouraged them to do so. Their reaction to the music was spontaneous. They made a harmonious choral of Frank Sinatra's "My Way."

On Lewis' final road trip, the one with GG, they had listened to music the entire time. When this song came on Lewis' playlist, he shared with GG that it was his favorite.

To savor the moment, they pulled the car over at one of the mountains overlook points. Lewis was of course photographing the scenery, and they had the song on replay mode.

It looped over and over. They both knew all the words and sang them loudly. That is when Lewis explained to GG that he knew his end was near, that he was facing the final curtain, but he was certain that he'd done it his way.

That moment was precious to GG and he had shared the story with all who would listen, including Evelyn. She would concur. She had heard Lewis blasting the song in the background when she would talk with him on the phone. He would exclaim that he had lived a full life with a few regrets but ultimately, he had done it his way.

She thought it appropriate to surprise GG and play that song as a tribute to Lewis and to their friendship. She had not given much thought to how Rev. Harris would react to it.

The Harrises looked straight ahead without speaking, without touching, without sharing. They sat together but grieved apart. It was their son's very public funeral service, and the world was watching them probably unaware that they were alone together.

She was pleased with the crowd's impromptu tribute to Lewis. She leaned slightly to see GG a few seats down and he nodded in appreciation.

Rev. Harris was livid.

What followed was a typical, Church of Christ Order of Funeral Service. The unique aspect of the Churches of Christ is that they have no governing offices or central organization. The churches were founded after the Civil War when differences in Bible interpretation sparked division within the Disciples of Christ Church.

Each church, such as NLKCCM, is autonomous. Its members look only to the Bible for guidance.

At the center of this teaching are the Scriptures, which are divinely inspired. One must immerse oneself in Christ to attain salvation. Members believe that Christian souls can enter paradise at death and the unfaithful are taken to Hell on Judgement Day, which happens with Jesus' Second Coming.

These are the doctrines that Rev. Harris holds to be true and, therefore, guide all the principles of his dogmatic life. Although Lewis did not agree with all aspects of his father's beliefs, he respected them, and he honored him.

The approved Order of Service (excluding that musical selection) was as follows: Processional, Prayer, Song (Hymn of Comfort), Poem, Old Testament Scripture, New Testament Scripture, Prayer, Obituary Reading, Eulogy, Benediction, Recessional, and Interment or Committal location.

All went according to plan. Well, almost all of it did. There was just this one thing before the Recessional. The camera zoomed in again to the bands.

Rev. Harris looked at Evelyn and spoke firmly through his gritted teeth, "Are those bands playing again!?"

Smugly, "Not exactly, Dear."

A moment later, a photo of Lewis and Patty appeared on the jumbotrons. Rev. Harris exclaimed, "I had forgotten that photo. Look at them! Look at our babies."

Evelyn had found it framed on the dresser in Patty's bedroom just a week ago, the day of the building collapse. In that snapshot, Lewis and Patty were little children, perhaps 7 and 8 years old, at a Christian summer camp. They had carved wooden crosses. Patty was delightedly smiling down at Lewis. His cross had won 1st place. He had not just carved as the other kids did, but forever the artist, he had added a purple drapery on his cross, and small nails where the hands and feet would have been. He also used splashes of red paint to symbolize bloodshed. He finished it off by etching a Scripture reference on his cross, "Matt 6:14".

In the photo, Lewis was smiling broadly for the camera and while holding the trophy with this left hand, he proudly held his cross close to his heart with his right hand. His cross was unlike any of the others.

Estelle was at a piano at center field. That sight warmed Evelyn's heart because now she understands why she has yearned piano all these years. It is in her bloodline. It is a part of who she is.

Estelle began to play and once again the lyrics scrolled on the screen, so the crowd sang along. This time it was a hymn. It was "The Old Rugged Cross", a popular song written in 1912 by the Evangelist George Bennard.

> *On a hill far away stood an old rugged cross*
> *The emblem of suffering and shame*

And I love that old cross
where the dearest and best
For a world of lost sinners was slain

So I will cherish the old rugged cross
Till my trophies at last I lay down
And I will cling to the old rugged cross
And exchange it some day for a crown

Rev. Harris murmured to Evelyn, "At least this one was a hymn, but the piano is garish."

To his surprise, Evelyn had not arranged for just any piano for her twin to play that day. It was a Bösendorfer Imperial Concert Grand piano that was handcrafted in Austria. It would retail for $560,000 in the U.S., and she had purchased it in memory of her darling son.

Evelyn whispered proudly to her husband, "I donated it to the Manhattan School of the Arts."

Irately, "I beg your pardon."

She repeated, "I purchased the piano and then donated it to the Manhattan School of the Arts. That is where Lewis wanted to study photography but was not permitted to do so."

She continued, "And that is where I will learn music theory and composition, beginning this spring."

"You'll begin what? Studying music at your age?"

"Oh, I will do much more than study it. I will compose classical arrangements, just like Chopin and

Beethoven. On that piano. In Lewis' memory. In the spring."

"Evelyn, no ..."

"Yes. I am doing it my way."

"I am appalled, Evelyn."

"You'll be fine, Patrick."

9. CONSOLATION

A couple of hours after Lewis' interment, Evelyn and Estelle, along with the convoy of 23 cars filled with loved ones were back on the road. Some turned off in New Jersey; some in Maryland and D.C.; and the others were driving back to Shen Valley. They were going back to Patty.

Ida was in the convoy, driving her car and speaking to Major Cory and General Pressley. They had attended the funeral and were en route to the airport to return to the west coast. She had confirmed their safe arrival to the airport when she received a text message from Officer Jack Goodleaf of Goodleaf Vineyard and Cellars.

"Hello Gorgeous."

She was intrigued. *"Hi there."*

"I am sorry I could not make the funeral. Are you on your way here?"

"Yes."

"Good. ETA?"

"I am not sure. I need to make a stop in D.C."

"How long will you be here?"

"A few days."

"Great. Can't wait to see you.

Ida wasn't the only one receiving text messages.

Dr. Ellis texted Evelyn, "I streamed the funeral service today. I thought it was beautiful. I am very sorry that I never got to meet Lewis."

She replied immediately, "Thank you. How's Patricia?"

"There's slight improvement. I'd like to run an idea by you."

"I am listening."

"Call me when you are back in the Valley?"

"Sure."

Rev. Harris received a text as well. *"Hello Sir, this is Mattie.*

"Hello."

Calculatedly, "I have papers I need you to sign tonight. May I bring them to your penthouse?"

"Affirmative."

"Great. I know you have guests. Perhaps after they leave?"

"2100hrs."

"Cool. I will call Phoebe when I arrive."

"I gave Phoebe the evening off. Call me when you arrive."

Thrilled, "Yes, Sir."

By 9:00 PM, Evelyn had arrived back to Patty's house. Estelle offered to stay with her, but she preferred to be alone. It had been a long day. She was drained both physically and emotionally. She had ridden roundtrip from Shen Valley to Manhattan and back, attended Lewis' funeral and burial services, faced her husband, and worried of Patty every minute. She had planned to call Dr. Ellis and get more details of Patty's rehab, but first she'd enjoy a hot bubble bath.

She had not cried.

With all Evelyn had endured over the past couple of weeks, she had not wept. She slid down into the warm, soothing, fragrance-filled water, until the suds reached her neck. She pondered, *What woman goes through what I am suffering and does not cry?*

She wondered if her grieving was normal, if perhaps she was in shock and this was an ordinary response to such devastating news. She questioned her feeling of numbness and wondered if more intense grief would come much later.

She recalled her last conversation with Lewis. She had told him how proud she was of him and how much she loved him. She was thankful for those last precious moments with him.

While she could not make up for lost time with Patricia, she could be there now. That helps. She could make sure that just as a mother deer fiercely protects and gently guides her feeble fawn, she would be there to do the same for Patty.

About Estelle, well, better late than never. They could bond now as twins do. They could have a sibling relationship. They could be friends.

She acknowledged that while Rev. Harris had kept a life-altering secret, he had done so thinking that he was being honorable. He had always loved her and provided for her and protected her. He had made a mistake. She did not feel their marriage was in jeopardy, but there certainly would be a few changes.

What really bothered Evelyn in that moment was her relationship with the Lord. She was angry with God. She was disappointed in Him. She decided to talk to Him about it.

Dear God,

I thank you for every day of the 43 years you blessed us with Lewis. I just wish we had more time. He was a delightful son, always cheerful, and very eager to please. His struggle was in the conflict between who he was and who his father wanted him to be. Thank you for blessing him in spite of those differences. And thank you for allowing Patrick to see just how much Lewis really admired him.

I thank you for Patricia. She is strong. She always has been. I think she gets her resilience from her father. I realize she has a long way to go in recovery, but I am not worried. You are Jehovah Rapha, the God who heals. You've done it before, and I know you will do it again. And I am just so very grateful that I can be here for her.

I thank you for Estelle. There has always been a void in my life, but I could not identify it. I could not put a name on it. A piece of me had always been missing. Thank you for filling that void. I am looking forward to heartfelt conversations with her. We have so much to share.

I thank you for Patrick. He has always been good to me. All these years that I have heard of horrible marital situations in other couples, they were never my own experiences. I have never had to worry about other women, dangerous vices, bad habits, domestic abuse, or even financial matters. He can be overbearing at times, but I can deal with that. He chose to honor my father's wish instead of being truthful to us, and I can forgive him for that because he thought he was doing the right thing.

My concern, Lord, is my relationship with you. Patrick is mere man, and so he is subject to fault. But you are sovereign. Nothing can happen without your permission.

How could you permit this? Why would you permit this? What good can come from so much pain?

I honor you, but I do not understand why you have allowed this nightmare to happen. I pray you make your plans known. I pray you reveal how all this can work together for the good to those of us who love you, to those of us who are the called according to your purpose.

Show me your purpose.

Amen.

As soon as Evelyn was out of the bathtub, she called Dr. Ellis.

He answered on the first ring, "Hello."

"Hello, Dr. Ellis."

"Thank you for calling. I'd like to run something by you."

She would have suggested they wait until morning, but if it concerned Patricia, then every minute mattered. Besides, she would rest better if there was any good news. "Sure."

"May I come over? It would be better in person."

"Here? Now? It is a little late, but I guess it is okay."

She quickly changed out of the pajamas she had just put on, and into yoga clothes. They were not as casual as nightclothes but much more comfortable than the black dress she had worn all day. She pulled hair up into a loose topknot and was just about to moisturize her face and hands when the doorbell rang. Typically, she would not have been so unpresentable for a guest, but he was just Patty's physician and there was something about him that was appeasing.

She opened the door and was immediately reminded of how handsome the doctor was. Of course, he was not as striking as her husband, nor as charming as her son that she had just buried, but he was still a welcomed sight.

He seemed a bit surprised, "You look amazing!"

"Thank you. I apologize that I am so casual."

"I like it. This is a nice look on you." He then looked toward the other rooms, "Is anyone else here?"

"No. I needed some time alone."

"I see. I won't stay long."

Pointing to the sofa, "Please sit. May I offer you something? Tea?"

"Sure. Tea would be nice."

He was scrolling through graphs on his iPad when she returned with the serving tray. She sat next to him on the sofa and found the smell of his cologne pleasing. Likewise, he enjoyed the fragrance from her bath oils.

He leaned in a little closer and held his tablet so she could see it. "Post-traumatic amnesia (PTA) is a state of confusion that occurs immediately following a traumatic brain injury (TBI). As is common with PTA, Patty is disoriented and unable to remember specific events. However, she does have some recall. She is also unable to state her name, where she is, and what time it is, but she can write them. She is communicating with us.

"This is encouraging. Is her condition permanent?"

"PTA may be either short term or longer lasting but is hardly ever permanent. I am hopeful that when her continuous memory returns, she can function normally."

"Okay. Are there any indications of which term Patty's condition is, short or long?"

"That is just it. A person who experiences a moderate TBI may have PTA from one to seven days following the traumatic event. A person with a severe TBI is likely to have PTA for more than seven days. Patty is at day number 12, so there is something I would like to try."

Sipping her herbal tea, "Please continue."

"We have a copy of the photo journal that Lewis created. We also have a recording of the funeral service today. I would like to show them to Patty."

"Wouldn't older photos, those from her childhood or college, be more effective?"

"Perhaps. But I have conducted extensive research on cognitive rehabilitation. There is a wide range of evidence to support interventions that incorporate post-injury photos to trigger memories."

"I don't understand."

"I am hopeful that photos from Lewis' journal and his funeral service will facilitate cognitive rehabilitation."

That did not make since to Evelyn. If the objective was to assist with memory recall, wouldn't it make more sense to use photos from before the accident? *Why not use photos from Patty's social media? Or from her photography collection of sunrises and sunsets? What he's suggesting sounds depressing.*

Evelyn did not disagree with him straightway though because he was the medical expert, "If you think it is helpful, I will think about it."

"She will need support. The more family and familiar faces the better."

"Of course. I will be there. Estelle, Ida, Ned, the Goodleafs, we can all be there. I will discuss it with them in the morning."

He noticed that her hands were trembling slightly, and she was yawning. "You have had a stressful day. I should leave."

At that moment, she had decidedly no longer wanted to be alone. "You could stay a few more minutes. It is fine."

"Okay." Looking across the room at Patty's small wine refrigerator, "Would you like a glass of wine? Perhaps it could help you relax?"

"Good idea." She stood to go get it, but he stopped her.

"Please. Allow me."

He poured them each just enough for a tasting. In two sips her glass was empty. "I think I would like a little more."

"Of course."

When she finished that tasting and then the next, it happened. Evelyn wept. The tears she had bottled-up all day finally made an appearance. They did not come out like a rushing flood though. They were not the uncontrollable streams she would have anticipated. They trickled.

Thankfully she was not crying alone. There was something about Dr. Ellis that comforted her. His presence offered her solace. He held her until she had cried herself to sleep. He did not let go even after she had drifted off. He propped his feet up on the cocktail table and allowed her to rest with her head on his chest, and his arms wrapped around her.

That is how they would be found when Ida arrived in the middle of the night, after her stopover in D.C.

At the same time that Evelyn was receiving her guest at Patty's cottage, Mattie was making her moves back at the penthouse. She called Rev. Harris.

"Sir, I am downstairs."

"Roger that. Sign in with an attendant. I am on my way."

This would be the first time the two of them met. She didn't get anywhere close to him at the funeral. The church staff had sat several rows behind those who processed into the stadium with the Harrises.

Mattie was glad that this encounter would be without Phoebe's interference. She had an agenda.

Rev. Harris was not prepared for what would step onto his elevator. Her appearance was vile.

She had heard that his favorite color was purple, so she dressed for him that evening. Her leather jacket, ponytail, eye shadow, lipstick, earrings, nail polish, sweater/dress, fishnet hose, heels, and hobo bag, were all purple.

When the elevator door opened, he waived her inside and said, "You look like a grape."

She took no offense, "I like purple."

"Obviously."

Once upstairs and inside the condo, the first room they reached was Phoebe's office. Mattie was surprised when they walked past it.

"I thought all transactions were in Phoebe's office."

"Phoebe's not here. I will review the documents in my parlor."

She smiled luminously.

He was polite. "May I offer you something while you wait?"

"A drink would be nice. What do you have?"

"Coffee, tea, water, ..."

She was hasty. "Nothing stronger? It is been a rough day."

He thought she was as tacky as she looked, but he remained mannerly. "We have wine."

"Where is it? I will get it while you read."

He pointed down a hallway. "There is a wine cellar at the end of the hallway."

She was happy to grab a bottle, "Do you have a preference?"

"It is my cellar. I like everything I stock."

Mattie opened a door to what appeared to be a closet converted into a wine cooler. It had space for 48 bottles, and more than half the spaces were filled. She imagined they were for festive cocktail parties, special occasions, and bottles to gift to friends.

She chose the 1858 Cabernet Sauvignon that Ida had just brought from Napa Valley. It was not the most expensive, at $70/bottle, but she was excited to taste it.

"Is this okay, Sir?"

"Yes. Please enjoy."

"Will you have a glass as well?"

"No, thank you."

She poured a full 13 oz glass and began to gulp. The hand-crafted Cab was a powerhouse in flavor and texture featuring luscious, ripe blackberry flavors with undertones of dark chocolate and toasted oak. "Oh, my goodness, this is delicious! You really should try it."

"I will pass. Thank you."

She changed her tactics. "The service was beautiful today."

He was obviously still irked about it, "Mostly."

Bingo! That was it. A door had opened. The entire church staff had been shocked about the music at the funeral. "Were you displeased, Sir?"

"I am not a fan of musical instruments in church."

"Then why did you agree to it?"

"I did not."

"I see." She decided to push just a little harder. "A man in your position should be respected. He was your son, your namesake. It did not seem, if you do not mind me saying, that it was appropriate to surprise you that way today."

"Exactly."

"I am sorry I did not get to meet Lewis. What was he like?"

Rev. Harris finally lifted his eyes from the documents and walked over to gaze at the skyline view through the enormous windows. He began to share his favorite of Lewis' childhood stories, the one about the cross at summer camp. At one moment, his voice slightly quivered.

Mattie, not one to miss an opportunity, poured him a glass of wine, kicked her shoes off, and sashayed to his side. Not realizing how much he was sipping, as one story led to another, Mattie made sure she kept his glass topped off. When they had finished the bottle, she announced, "I am happy to stay a little longer and keep you company, Sir."

He recalled the pain and the loneliness of the first night he was home without Evelyn and chose to extend her visit. "I appreciate that. Thank you."

"Sure. We need food to soak up some of this alcohol. Which way is the kitchen?"

He pointed.

"I'll whip us something up. Can you grab another bottle?"

She was a little brash and more impetuous than he would have preferred, but her company was so much better than being alone that night. "Sure."

The companionship must have been adequate because they fell asleep, him on one end of the sofa, and her nearby with her feet in his lap. That is where Phoebe would find them when she returned to work in just a few hours.

10. Conspiracy

Ida had been talking on the phone with Officer Goodleaf for most of her ride down to Shen Valley. He was actually a pretty good conversationalist, particularly about the wines from his family's vineyard, and great virtual company for her road trip.

That would explain why she had not felt compelled to respond to the numerous texts from Major Cory. She was contemplating that whole MCCES situation when she turned into Patty's driveway and saw a different car there.

It was odd that in the middle of the night, there would be a car other than Patty's or Estelle's. *Who was there visiting with Evelyn at such a late hour?* There was something sobering about that scenario. Ida was hoping there was not more bad news.

She mentioned it to Officer Goodleaf who was still on the phone and he asked if he should come over.

"No, thanks. I'm good."

"Let me know when you are inside that everything is okay."

"I will. I'll call you back."

She eased up the walkway to the front door. When she gently turned the knob, it opened with ease. It is not uncommon to leave Patty's door unlocked because the only nearby neighbors are the Goodleafs.

When she entered, the scene made her gasp. What was happening? There were empty wine bottles lying on the coffee table with two glasses. Evelyn was in workout clothes with her hair pinned up, which was fine. Her legs were crossed with her feet on the cocktail table, which never would have happened. According to Evelyn, it is abominable to put one's feet on a table. She would exclaim that, "It is a table, not an ottoman." Her head was on Dr. Ellis' chest.

What is even more astonishing is that Evelyn was asleep with a tissue box in her lap and used tissues all around her. She had clearly been crying.

He, too, was asleep. His feet were also on the cocktail table. His head was tilted all the way back, resting on the back of the sofa and his mouth was slightly opened. Both his arms embraced Evelyn.

Ida was trying to imagine what had transpired. *Well, they are fully clothed. That is a good thing. Okay, so maybe he stopped by to pay his respects given that he did not attend Lewis' funeral service, and maybe he offered to console Evelyn, and they dozed off. Yeah, that's it.*

She received a text from Officer Goodleaf. "Everything okay?"

She stepped outside and called him. "I think everything is okay, but I am not sure."

"What's up?"

"Dr. Ellis is here. He is asleep in the living room. Should I awake them?"

"Dr. Ellis?"

"Yes."

"From the rehab?"

"Yes."

"Oh no."

"What's wrong?"

"It could be nothing but he's on probation at the rehab. His position is interim while they complete a background check, and rumor has it that they have found some discrepancies. They are conducting an investigation. This is a very small town so word spreads quickly."

"He is under investigation, overseeing Patty's care, and now he is cozy with Mrs. Harris."

"Interesting."

"Thanks. I've gotta go."

"I can come over."

"Nope, I'm good. I'll call you later. I might need more wine."

Ida walked back into the house and this time instead of politely clearing her throat she shouted their names, "Dr. Ellis, Mrs. Harris."

Both were startled and they jumped.

"Good morning", she said and still slightly louder than a polite greeting would have sounded.

Evelyn leapt to her feet, "Oh dear."

Dr. Ellis did the same. "My apologies. I should leave."

Suspicious of his motives, Ida held the door open for him in full agreement with his decision to leave.

Evelyn began to scramble to clean the room, clearing glasses and bottles and tissues.

Ida intervened. "Mother Harris, you can turn in. I will take care of it."

"No, no. I've got it."

Ida insisted, "You need rest. I am happy to take care of it."

What neither of them knew was that there was a similar scene about to unfold in the penthouse.

Sometimes Phoebe stays in her suite in the Harrises' home. It is convenient because her workdays are often very long. But she maintains her apartment near her family on Long Island and frequently stays there for rest and relaxation. She had been so attentive to Rev. Harris' needs since his return from Shen Valley that he had insisted she take a night off and be with her family. Immediately following the funeral, she took him up on his offer but assured him that she would return first thing in the morning.

True to her word, she stepped off the elevator before daylight. She placed her things in her office and was expecting to find Rev. Harris having coffee in his parlor and anticipating the sunrise.

He was indeed in the parlor, but with Mattie. There were empty wine bottles and food containers and pillows were strewn about. It looked as if a party had gone horribly wrong. She shouted, "Good morning!"

They jumped.

Rev. Harris appeared disoriented. He scanned the room trying to piece together the events of the prior evening.

Phoebe gave him a nod toward the stairs, politely suggesting that he leave the room and his guest for her to contend with.

Mattie began grabbing all her purple stuff: shoes, bag, jacket, and her ponytail that she had laid out perfectly on the coffee table to preserve its tangle-free texture.

When she stood to face Phoebe, she was only wearing one earring. It was a huge purple chandelier that clipped on and reached down to her shoulder.

"Where is your other earring?" Phoebe asked impatiently.

Mattie thought she had purposefully placed her earrings with the ponytail, but she was wearing one and the other was now misplaced. "Oh no, my earring. These are my favorite purple earrings and I am missing one."

"Housekeeping will be here soon to restore order to this room. I will make sure they look for it and we will return it to you promptly."

Mattie took the hint. "Fine, I'll leave."

"Follow me please." Phoebe escorted Mattie to the elevator but did not call for a security escort. She chaperoned her onto the elevator, through the lobby all the way to the doorman, and then asked that he assist Mattie with transportation: a cab, an Uber, or something.

Once Mattie was in her car, she texted Dr. Ellis. "The manager walked in on us, but I got the photos before she came in. Did you?"

He replied, "Yep. Ida walked in on us, but I got photos, too."

Mattie was having second thoughts, "Rev. Harris is actually a nice guy. I kind of feel bad about this."

Dr. Ellis stopped texting and called her. Dropping the fake British accent, "We have a plan. This is the perfect opportunity."

"I know. It's just that Rev. Harris has been through so much, and he is so sad. And are you sure you are comfortable doing this to Evelyn? None of this feels right."

"They're rich. They'll be fine. Just stick with the plan. We are almost done."

Reluctantly, she agreed. "Okay."

"I have to go make rounds at the rehab. I will call you later."

"Be careful. Don't get caught."

The morning did not get much better.

Phoebe had refilled her coffee cup and was just about to call the church about Mattie. She wanted to know what happened to the original EA and how the company vetted new employees. Mattie's appearance and mannerisms should have been grounds to decline her for this position.

She had picked up her phone when a lobby attendant called up to her. He had received a special delivery for Rev. Harris. It was a small envelope.

"Please bring it up."

Phoebe opened it to find photos inside. There was also a note, "Transfer $250,000 into this bank account or Monday's news headline will read: *Grieving Pastor Enjoys Purple Passion.*" The photos could not have been staged more cleverly. Wine bottles, a passed-out Rev. Harris, and the woman in purple posing in highly suggestive positions. Mattie had framed Rev. Harris and was now blackmailing him.

In the meantime, a courier brought a similar envelope to Patty's home. Ida signed for it. It was addressed to Mrs. Harris, but Ida had been assisting with the paperwork for Patty's medical services and Lewis's funeral, and she thought this might be related.

There were photos looking much worse than the scene Ida discovered. Clearly, they had been staged. The note read, "Transfer $250,000 into this bank account or Monday's headline will read: *Mourning Mother and her Daughter's Doctor.*"

Ida texted Phoebe. "Houston, we have a problem."

Phoebe replied, "There is a fire burning here as well."

"Mrs. Harris is asleep, but I will go out to my car and call you."

"Rev. Harris is asleep, but I will close my office door."

On that private call, they shared the details of the threats and compared their observations and then they knew that the thief had come to steal and to kill and to destroy. He had formed weapons against them when they were most vulnerable.

Phoebe and Ida decided to hire the Harrises' private investigator to discover exactly who the imposters were so they could plan how best to respond.

Before they hung up, Ida had an idea. "Did you find the other purple earring?"

"Yes, it was between the sofa cushions."

"Great. I need it. I will also need a few things from my lab. Can you help me get an overnight delivery here?"

Phoebe was not sure what Ida's plan was, but she had confidence that it would be a good one. "Sure."

Ida would have about 24 hours before receiving the package from Phoebe. That is ample time to plan. The uniqueness of her electronics designs is due to how she lays out the electrical circuits and decides how they will work. The first thing she would need is printed circuit boards (PCBs). That means she would need her PCB design software tools. She would have all she needed on her laptop and with the equipment that Phoebe would send, this plan just might work.

She grabbed her laptop from her car and made coffee. It would be a long 24 hours.

Anyone could Google *listening devices* or *hidden voice recorders,* and purchase some to try and trap Dr. Ellis and Mattie, but Ida had something more specific in mind. She would need to not only record conversations but to also expose them without disparaging Rev. and Mrs. Harris' reputations.

There would be several obstacles. First, if they recorded Mattie's voice, there is no way of proving who she was speaking to. Second, there are at least 200 miles between Ian and Mattie, so the only way to capture both of them would be to tap their phones, but they are probably using disposable phones. Third, they would have to both be exposed at the same time to avoid release of the photos by either of them. Finally, they are expecting cash deposits in 24 hours, but Ida would not have her package from Phoebe until then.

After a few hours of work, she had a detailed plan. She needed some more equipment and the cooperation of Mrs. Harris.

At that perfect moment, Evelyn had awakened and entered the kitchen. She was surprised to see Ida's laptop, notes, and sketches scattered on the kitchen table.

"How long have you been awake?"

"A while. Pull up a seat, Mother Harris."

Evelyn joined Ida at the table for coffee. Ida showed her the photos that had been delivered, shared the details of her plan, and then came to the part where she needed assistance.

Evelyn, as unruffled as usual, "I was suspicious of Mattie from the first phone call. She does not fit on the church team. And now she is blackmailing my husband the day after our son's funeral."

Ida was typing fast but was still able to respond, "Phoebe is looking into how Mattie got the job."

Evelyn continued, still unflustered, "And Dr. Ellis did not quite add up either. Some of his suggestions for Patty did not make sense."

Ida added, "He sure is fine though. Too bad he is not real."

Evelyn ignored that remark.

"I am designing a listening device and need you to plant it in his car. Also, I need an additional 24 hours."

Evelyn was sipping the hot coffee and did not put the cup down but peered over the rim to Ida. "How am I supposed to do that?"

Never looking up from her laptop, "More of whatever happened last night, Ma'am."

"Nothing happened. He feels more like a friend than some romantic entanglement."

Still intently dragging her finger across the touchpad of her laptop, she suggested, "When you go to visit Patty at rehab this morning, discretely see him in his office. Tell him that you cannot get access to the money without your husband's permission. The reason is that after the piano incident he froze your accounts. That should buy us another day."

Evelyn understood. "I'll get dressed and head over there now."

While Evelyn was in the shower, Ida called Phoebe.

"Hi, Phoebe. Were you able to find everything?"

"Yes. The package will arrive tomorrow morning."

"Great. When I receive it, I will plant a miniature bug in it and return it to you. I need you to figure out a way to make sure she wears it."

Phoebe questioned, "How shall I do that?"

"I do not know. You'll have to figure that out, but she must be wearing it when she calls Dr. Ellis because it has to be close to her mouth for clear recording."

"Okay. I will think of something."

Finally, Ida needed to make another call.

He answered formally, "Good Morning, this is Major Cory."

"Hi there."

He sounded hopeful. "Ida, it's good to hear from you. I've been texting."

"I know. I have a proposition for you."

"I like it already."

"No, not like that. I am working on an urgent project, a critical mission. I need equipment that I cannot access immediately. Could I give you a list and ask you to overnight a few items to me from MCCES? And to keep this between us?"

"Ida, you have been ignoring my texts and calls."

"Yeah, sorry about that."

"But now you need a favor? And one that could potentially jeopardize my career?"

"To the contrary, it might help your career. I am designing a prototype of a pair of communications devices. If I use MCCES equipment and I am an MCCES consultant, then MCCES will own the patents. It is a win-win. I think it is actually what General Pressley is hoping for. And I really need your help."

"So, if I send you this equipment and your invention works, I will deliver it to my boss."

"Exactly."

"And you won't need to come out here and work in California. You can design more new devices from the east coast."

"Perhaps."

He was catching on, "It sounds like I may never see you again." He was wondering if he had done or said something wrong.

Ignoring his feelings, she was focused, "But this new prototype may get you a promotion."

He conceded, "Send me your list. I will overnight a package to you."

"Thank you."

She was anxiously swiping between the various images on her laptop, blueprints on her iPad, and the calculator on her phone. She was jotting notes and numbers with pen and paper. She was working frantically on the designs when suddenly, she began to have a headache.

That is when Ida realized she had been at it for several hours and needed rest. Just as Evelyn was leaving for the rehab center, Ida decided to shower and nap in hopes of relief from the now intensifying headache, and then resume with a fresh start.

11. COMMUNICATIONS

She was resting well in Patty's bed and must have slept for a while because the next thing she recalled was Evelyn waking her.

"Ida. Ida. Ida, wake up."

"Hi. What time is it? When did you get back?"

"It is late afternoon. I visited with Patricia until Dr. Ellis' shift ended and then I was able to speak with him."

Ida's headache was not completely gone. She sat up slowly and was holding her forehead in the palm of her hand. "How's Patty?"

"She is better and staying awake longer. She is not yet speaking but she is writing more with questions and requests. And she seems comfortable."

"What kind of questions and requests?"

"Well, for one, she asked if there is an attic and an old Bible. When I confirmed, she asked if I would bring it to her."

Ida looked up with elation, "She remembers that her old Bible is in the attic?"

Evelyn nodded slowly, "Yes. Thank God. She has finally remembered something long-term."

"That is great. I will take it over to her. And Lewis' summer camp cross is up there with it, the one that's in the photo. I will take that as well since she kept them together."

Then Ida inquired about Dr. Ellis, "And the doctor, how did that go?"

"I met with him. He has no shame. There is no shock factor, no remorse. It is as if he has no conscience. He seems to feel entitled."

"Yeah, he is a con artist, a professional."

"He didn't even speak in the British accent."

"Not surprising. He was too good to be true."

"Anyway, I convinced him that I could do nothing on a Sunday evening, and that I will call Patrick first thing tomorrow morning. It will then take another 24 hours for me to have access to funds. So, we have until Tuesday morning."

"Okay. So that solves one problem. It buys us time with the payment on this end. But they will still expect Rev. Harris' deposit tomorrow morning. We need to delay the time for that one. Let's call Phoebe."

There was something Evelyn did not want to say, but it would be best so she blurted it out, "I think we should inform Patrick."

Ida recalled how advantageous his command was when searching for Patty, but she was still disgusted with Rev. Harris, so she opposed. "I do not want his help."

Evelyn was much more objective, "I am hurt, Ida. What he has done is unthinkable, but we are a family, and we are under attack. Patrick is a warrior and mighty at battle."

Evelyn's logic was sound, so Ida assented, "Okay. Let's call Phoebe."

Phoebe answered on the first ring. "Hi, Ida."

"Hi, Phoebe."

"I am here with Mrs. Harris. She feels we should inform Rev. Harris."

This came as a relief to Phoebe who was not comfortable keeping such a secret from Rev. Harris, "He is in the parlor. Please hold."

Phoebe rushed into the parlor to inform him that there was an urgent call from Ida and Mrs. Harris.

A couple of minutes later Phoebe unmuted her phone and spoke again, "We are here together in the parlor. You are on speaker phone. Please continue."

Ida responded, "We are here at Patty's, Mrs. Harris and me. You are on speaker as well."

Rev. Harris anxiously ordered, "Situation report!"

Ida briefed him on Mattie, Dr. Ellis, and the photos. She also shared her plan for the new bugging devices.

He was tracking her every word and nodding in approval as she spoke. He did not interrupt her. He was grateful that she had a good plan.

He could deal with purple Mattie's scam. Many have tried before her. He could have easily called the authorities as he had done with previous extortion attempts over the years. This time was different.

He was furious. He wanted to handle this one himself. Specifically, the medical imposter who was pretending to care for Patty, who timed his scam to align with Lewis' funeral, and even worse, tried to manipulate Evelyn. That man had made a grave mistake plotting against Rev. Harris' family.

Rev. Harris called out, "Evelyn, how are you, Darling?"

At the sound of his voice, she began to weep. It was not the same as the cry she'd had with Dr. Ellis. This was different.

It was similar to his episode that first night he was back in the penthouse without her. Her emotions overtook her and began to cause a physical effect. She started having palpitations. She began sweating. Her mouth dried. She was hyperventilating. She could see Ida's mouth moving but she could not hear anything. And then the room started spinning.

Ida was calling her name, "Mother Harris, Mother Harris", and trying to calm her, but it was not working. Evelyn was in distress. She wanted to respond but could not. She wanted to move but was motionless.

Ida informed Rev. Harris and Phoebe that she was calling for a paramedic.

Rev. Harris sang out, "I am on my way, Evelyn. Hang in there, Darling."

And then to Phoebe, have Ralph drive me to the executive's airport. I need a flight to Virginia, now."

"Sir, it is Sunday evening. There are no more flights out tonight."

"Then Ralph has to drive me. Inform Ida that I will be there in 4 hours, and we can talk while I am in the car. We need to flesh out her plan."

"Yes, Sir." Phoebe was encouraged to see that he had returned to himself. His tone was stern. His look was determined. His eyes were strong. He was back in control.

"Phoebe, call my private investigator. Have him expedite his research. I need the file on Mattie and Dr. Ellis, pronto. Then get him on a call with Ida and me. We need to know everything about these charlatans."

"Roger that, Sir!"

In full command Rev. Harris' directives continued, "Call Estelle and have her go to Evelyn. She needs her sister. Also, call Ned and explain to him that we need a 24-hour security detail on Patty just in case Dr. Ellis tries something shady."

"Yes, Sir. Shall I notify the temp agency that we no longer need Mattie's services."

"Not yet. We do not want to do anything that would alert her to our status. Let her think I am still here in the penthouse for now. That will work to our advantage."

As he headed for the elevator to meet Ralph downstairs at the car, Phoebe shouted, "Sir, I will be praying for Mrs. Harris."

"Good. And pray for Dr. Ellis as well. He'll need it when I get my hands on him."

12. SOMETHING HAPPENED

The paramedics arrived to assist Evelyn. They examined her and determined that she was not experiencing a cardiac event and was not in imminent danger. It was probably a panic attack and she would be okay, but they recommended a trip to the hospital emergency room just in case.

Evelyn resisted initially. The thought of returning to that hospital after all they had endured was too much for her. She promised to rest and take it easy, and to reconsider if things were different when her husband arrived.

Estelle had entered the cottage at the same time as the paramedics. Ida filled her in on the scam that predicated this panic attack. Estelle was incensed and was resolute that she would not leave her sister's side until this matter was resolved. She also insisted they go to the hospital and have tests run to ensure Evelyn was not in danger. "Better safe than sorry, Sister. Let's go and have them verify you are okay."

Evelyn acquiesced.

Ida was not sure if the hospital would admit Evelyn and keep her overnight, or if they would run a few tests and then release her. She agreed to follow the ambulance and stay informed so she would have updates when Rev. Harris called.

Unfortunately, she still had the headache. It seemed a good idea to wait in her car in the hospital parking lot while they triaged Evelyn. She could let the windows down and enjoy the fresh mountain air.

It was peaceful. There were no sounds. Even in a hospital parking lot, there were no sirens, no car horns, no helicopters, nor any of the other sounds outside her condo in New York. Shen Valley was serene. She could see what Patty loved about it.

Deep breaths were helping but she still could not feel herself calming nor the headache easing up. The last time she was out there she had prayed, and it helped. She thought she'd try it again now.

Dear God,

It is me, Ida. I want to pray but truthfully, I do not know what to say. I should thank you for sparing me when I was here before. Do you remember the bear? Thanks for not letting it eat us! And for saving Patty, thanks so much for that, too. I have not forgotten those things.

I'm grateful, but every time I think we are over one obstacle, there is yet another one. Life is hard. Is it true that you won't put more on us than we can handle?

There is so much that I do not understand. Why did you allow those twins to be separated? Did you approve of Rev. Harris keeping secrets all those years? How did you choose to spare Patty but not Lewis? How did you determine the timing for the MCCES call? Why would you let Dr. Ellis and Mattie do this to the Harrises?

And my biggest question is, God, why am I in the middle of all of this?

I'm at a lost. Why me?

I don't have a specific request of you because I do not understand what's happening. I do not know what to ask for right now. I just know I need you to do something.

That's it.

That is all I've got.

Lord, please do something.

Ida could not think of anything else to say so she started singing the hymn that her grandmother used to sing. Grandma would sing it when she did her house chores. While cooking or cleaning, she'd sing that one song:

Father, I stretch my hand to thee. No other help I know. If thou withdraw thy hand from me, O, whither shall I go?

Ida smiled as she thought, *I think that must have been my grandmother's prayer: "Lord, please do something."*

She kept singing that one verse over and over until she sang herself to sleep in her car.

When she awakened, the first thing she did was check her phone. There was no call from Rev. Harris yet, which meant that he was still awaiting the report from the investigator. He would call to strategize as soon as he received the intel.

The chaplain approached Ida's car.

He said, "Ida, come to chapel."

"Excuse me?" She recognized him from the week before, when Patty was in this hospital.

He repeated softly, "Ida, come to chapel."

Then he walked away.

She was irate and thought, *Really, God? Are you kidding me?*

She began to speak aloud in her rapid speech. "I do not feel like going to chapel. I flew from California back to New York, attended Lewis' funeral, drove down to Virginia, designed schemes for new bugging devices, attended to Mrs. Harris, and now I am tired. I am sitting here in the dark in my car because my head hurts. I sat here and poured my heart out to you, God. I pleaded with you, 'Lord, please do something', and all I get in response is, 'Ida, go to chapel?'

She was irritated and she was disappointed, but she was curious. *How did the chaplain know she was there sitting alone in her car? Why would he invite her to chapel?*

She was intrigued, so she went.

When she approached the chapel, she could hear music inside. There was some sort of service or program taking place. She remembered a story written by Alex Haley in 1980 about the gospel singer, Mahalia Jackson. The singer had told Mr. Haley that in the concerts she poured everything in her out. Then she told him, 'Them little places where I started, they're my filling stations.' Ms. Jackson would slip in and sit on the back row of churches in disguise. When she was incognito, no one recognized her and therefore would not request her to sing. She would fill up at those services.

Ida decided to slip in and sit on the back row like Mahalia Jackson. She thought she might fill up if no one recognized her or called her out.

Just as she sat down, the chaplain announced that everyone should take a moment and greet someone else.

Ida was already annoyed. *Oh, Lord. Please do not make me have to talk to anyone. I do not feel like talking to anyone.*

A lady at the front of the chapel was hugging people and made eye contact with Ida.

Ida was even more irritated. *Oh, God, please no. Please do not let her come back here. I do not feel like hugging anyone.*

The lady pressed her way through the crowd. Her eyes were still locked on Ida.

Ida was maddening at that point. *I do not want to be greeted. I do not feel like meeting her.*

The lady finally reached Ida all the way on the back row. She was much older and much shorter than Ida.

Ida was riled. *I do not want to hug the little ole short lady who smells like peppermint.*

The lady reached up and hugged Ida and she whispered in her ear, "God heard you."

Ida froze.

The lady continued, "Everything is going to be alright, Ida. Trust in the Lord."

Ida was still motionless. It was time for the hug to end. People were returning to their seats. The music had stopped. Ida could not let go. She held the lady close and she could not let go.

When she finally released their embrace, she said to the lady, who was making her way back to her seat at the front of the chapel, "Something just happened."

The lady smiled and kept walking.

Ida said it again but shouted this time, "Something happened!"

Just then she heard the chaplain speak. His voice was that same kind one that had invited her to the chapel. He appealed to the congregants, "Is there anyone here in the need of prayer?"

Ida yelled out from the back row, "Me!" She raised her hand high and started waving it to get his attention.

And she sounded like an 8-year-old in a school classroom. "Ooh! Ooh! Me! Pick me! I need prayer. Me! It's me. It's me, standing in the need of prayer."

He made eye contact with her.

Ida trampled over the people at the end of her pew, ran up the aisle to the front of the chapel, and asked him to pray for her. The little ole lady and some others formed a circle around her. They each placed a hand on her, and they prayed.

Ida could hear them praying but their voices seemed far away. At some point, her feet began to move in a rhythm but there was no music playing. Soon something started rumbling in her belly and came out in forceful yet melodic sounds.

It was all so uncontrollable. If she could have, she would have stopped it and not made a scene. If she could have, she would have resumed her incognito status on that back row. If she could have, she would have stopped all of what was happening.

But she could not.

The Lord was doing something.

13. REVELATION

The prayer service ended, and Ida left the chapel to go and check on Evelyn. The tests results verified that Evelyn was not in danger and therefore the hospital was soon releasing her.

At that very moment, Ida received the text from Rev. Harris. She was able to report that they would all be back to Patty's cottage by the time he and Ralph arrived.

It was the middle of the night. They could all get a good rest and have a full day of planning before dealing with the scammers.

On her way back to her car, random songs from the chapel service kept coming back to Ida:

Amazing Grace.

What a Friend we have in Jesus.

Because He lives.

It was the last song that resonated. It was that one that summed up her experience:

He touched me. And oh, the joy that floods my soul! Something happened, and now I know He touched me, and made me whole.

Ned was securing Patty's room, which no one thought odd because of their relationship. He would not leave her side. Desperately wanting her to recover, he prayed for a miracle. He prayed without ceasing, all night long. Having waited all those years for her father's approval, Jacob Nedfeather still had not given up on their love.

The investigator discovered the true identities of Dr. Ellis and Mattie, and he had provided a full brief to Rev. Harris and Ida. They now knew the reason for the scam.

Ida would receive the packages from Phoebe and Major Cory and assemble the devices the following morning. She and Rev. Harris could work out the details of the sting during that time.

Rev. and Mrs. Harris were asleep in the spare bedroom, together. It would be the first good night's sleep either of them had since the earthquake.

Ralph was asleep out on the front porch, partly because he enjoyed the night air, but also because he was armed and prepared for unexpected visitors should there be any. He stood watch.

Estelle was asleep on the sofa. She was resting among family.

Ida was in Patty's bed, still singing the hymn from the chapel service, *Something happened and now I know, He touched me and made me whole.*

At exactly 6:14 AM on Monday, FedEx rang the doorbell. Both packages had arrived from Phoebe and Major Cory.

Ida worked fervently on the miniature devices for several hours. One would be planted in the purple earring and returned to Phoebe today. Phoebe would drive halfway from New York, and so would Ralph from Virginia. That way they'd both only be driving two hours each way to meet in the middle, and they could get a kiss at the purple earring handoff.

The plan was finalized. Phoebe would invite Mattie over to pick up her earring early on Tuesday along with an envelope from Rev. Harris. In the envelope would be a note explaining that an electronic transfer of that size is not possible without triggering the IRS, so the transaction was in cash. What Phoebe would not tell her is that they had arranged for counterfeit bills.

Not knowing that Rev. Harris was in town or that Evelyn had a health scare, Dr. Ellis would still be expecting his payment. Evelyn would request to meet him and give him cash and use the same IRS excuse. She would prefer to meet in his car where there would be no witnesses to the transaction. Of course, once in his car, she would plant the miniature microphone (it looked like a button) that would broadcast his conversations.

By sunset, the plan was settled, the earring was done, and the button was completed. The family would enjoy dinner, compliments of the Goodleafs, and a relaxing evening. When the Goodleafs brought the food, their nephew, the Officer, accompanied them in hopes of connecting with Ida.

"Ida, Ida, Ida", he chanted. "I brought your favorite wine."

She politely declined, "Thank you, but I don't have a taste for wine this evening."

The family was shocked. Ida declined wine! *When did Ida not have a taste for wine?*

Officer Goodleaf tried another idea, "Well, I could stay and keep you company for a while", he offered.

That suggestion was not appealing to Ida either, "Thanks, but I'd rather not this evening."

That night the family rested well in the cozy little cottage surrounded by green pastures and the still waters of the Shenandoah River.

By morning, they were restored. Although they were preparing to confront evil, they were not fearful. They were comforted. Everything they needed had been provided to overcome the snares of their enemies. Surely, everything would work out for their good.

At dawn, the plan was in motion. Mattie was on her way to pick up her earring and envelope from Phoebe. Evelyn was en route to deliver the payment to Ian.

Phoebe had asked Mattie to wear a purple outfit again, including the earring because Rev. Harris liked it. If his schedule permitted, he would try to see her when she stopped by.

As soon as Mattie received her earring, she put it on. Phoebe handed her an envelope with the fake money in it and expressed regret that Rev. Harris would not be able to see her after all.

In exchange Mattie handed Phoebe an envelope with the memory card containing the photos and a note ensuring there were no copies. She was also apologetic. She seemed repentant during the transaction.

Phoebe was confused. *Could Mattie have been naïve enough to believe the transaction was not recorded? There are security cameras throughout the penthouse. And if she was so remorseful, why do this?*

Once she was back in her Uber, Mattie called Dr. Ellis. He had just met with Evelyn and was still in his car counting the money, not realizing they were counterfeit bills. Unlike the penthouse, in his car there were no security cameras, but their voices were being recorded. Evelyn had cleverly dropped the button mic near him.

When their conversation ended, Officer Goodleaf, tapped on Dr. Ellis' car window. He stated politely, "Sir, I need you to come with me."

"I beg your pardon?" Dr. Ellis was confounded.

"Let's go inside."

"Where?"

"Patty's room."

Dr. Ellis was not being arrested so he assumed he was probably not incriminated. He complied. "Sure thing."

When they reached Patty's room, he was surprised to find her entire family there and this time including Rev. Harris.

Back to his British accent, "What is going on?"

Rev. Harris walked up to him and stood nose to nose. "It is taking all my restraint to not break every bone in your skinny little body. You would be the one needing rehab."

Dr. Ellis did not respond to Rev. Harris. He took a few steps back from him, looked at Evelyn, and repeated, "What is going on?"

She said simply, "It is over. We know everything."

"What exactly do you know?"

Rev. Harris began to speak but Evelyn spoke up over him, "We know that when our mother was pregnant with us and our father was in the military, he had an affair. We know that his mistress was very young and emotionally unstable. She threatened to harm our mother if he didn't leave her."

Evelyn was becoming emotional, so Estelle helped with the reveal, "On the night of the car crash, our mother passed out and when she awakened, she had given birth, but she only knew of one baby, me. She did not know about Evelyn."

Estelle held Evelyn's hand as she continued, "Our father left a note that he would not be back. He took

Evelyn and fled the young mistress for a new life. He left our mother and me, without explanation."

Dr. Ellis was not surprised that they had finally figured it out, but still had the audacity to ask, "What does that have to do with me?"

Estelle answered, "Our father's young mistress was your mother. She was pregnant with you when he left her. And she loved him so much that she gave you his name. Your name is not Ian. It's *John, Jr.*, after our father. You are our half-brother."

All he could think to say was, "Good for you. You figured it out."

Evelyn needed answers, "He left our mother. He left your mother. Why would you blackmail me? Because he chose me?"

He was quick, "You had a beautiful life. He made sure you were well cared for, but not me. He gave me nothing. He left me nothing."

Ida asked, "Are you really a doctor? And what's with the fake British accent?"

He curtly responded, "I attended medical school in London, but I ran out of money and was not able to graduate."

"And how'd you get this job", one of them asked.

"Based on my research of post-traumatic amnesia, I was able to request this assignment with a forged license."

Rev. Harris asked, "And why did you drag purple Mattie into this?"

He might as well explain, "I needed an accomplice. She's my little sister. Our mother was committed to a mental institution shortly after Mattie was born. I've always looked after her."

Rev. Harris announced, "You didn't do such a great job."

Dr. Ellis (John Jr.) rebutted, "You've made a few mistakes yourself, or have you forgotten them?"

Rev. Harris in all of his anger retorted, "If you were not their brother, I'd have you and Grape Girl arrested."

Arrogantly, "Arrested for what? There is no evidence of a crime."

Ida spoke up, "Actually, there is. There's a recording device on her and one with you. Both recorded your conversation to the cloud. The time stamps of both will correlate. The devices also have GPS built in so we can trace locations at the time of the recordings. We can triangulate time, location, and conversation."

Astounded, "You bugged us? That cannot be legal. It won't hold up in a court."

Ida proudly responded again, "Actually, it is. This was a test of a prototype developed for the U.S. military, approved by General Phillip Pressley. You can fight them in court if you question authenticity."

"So, you want us to return the money?"

Evelyn said, "No. It is counterfeit. Just do not try to use it or you will be arrested."

She then presented his other option, "Brother, my hope is that we can start afresh."

She then addressed everyone in the room, including her husband, "We are a family. What's best for all of us is forgetting those things which are behind and straining toward what is ahead, a family made whole."

A nurse entered the room to administer Patty's medication. She gently placed a hand on her to awaken her.

Patty sat up and her eyes scanned the people in the room. She recognized them and she spoke for the first time, calling all their names, "Mother, Daddy, Ida, Ned, Dr. Ellis, Jillian, what's going on?"

Then, she realized she had fallen asleep clutching Lewis' wooden cross. She asked, "Where is Lewis?"

The family would have to fill her in on Lewis' story and all that followed.

The nurse gave a quick glance and sly smile to Ida.

Ida recognized her, "You're the lady from the chapel service on Sunday!"

The lady looked perplexed.

Ida clarified, "You're the lady who hugged me in the chapel program on Sunday evening. You placed a hand on me during prayer like you just did Patty."

The nurse continued to smile, and she exited the room without replying.

Jillian, Patty's roommate reacted, "Ida, there are no chapel services here on Sunday evenings."

ABOUT THE AUTHOR

Dr. Shawn Jones Richmond is an author of contemporary Christian fiction. Her books are designed to entertain and to draw people closer to God.

She is a speaker, teacher, and preacher.

She would be honored to facilitate a book discussion, Bible study, church service, or conference session for your group.

Connect with her at DrShawnRichmond.com.

And, stay tuned for her next book, "In the Presence of My Enemies", coming Summer 2021.

Made in the USA
Middletown, DE
07 April 2023

28181153R00086